by Lionel Derrick

PINNACLE BOOKS   **NEW YORK**

PENETRATOR #52: BROTHERHOOD OF BLOOD

Copyright © 1983 by Pinnacle Books

All rights reserved, including the right to reproduce this book or portions thereof in any form.

An original Pinnacle Books edition, published for the first time anywhere.

Special Acknowledgement to Chet Cunningham.

First printing, October 1983

ISBN: 0-523-41957-0

Can. ISBN: 0-523-43054-X

Cover illustration by George Wilson

Printed in the United States of America

PINNACLE BOOKS, INC.
1430 Broadway
New York, New York 10018

9 8 7 6 5 4 3 2 1

BROTHERHOOD
OF BLOOD

1

$5 Can Waste You

Something was wrong. Deadly wrong. Whatever it was made the short hairs on the nape of Mark Hardin's neck stand up—because he didn't know what was the problem.

He walked in from a vigorous ocean swim, knee-deep in the incoming and receding Pacific waves, toward world-famous Black's Beach in San Diego. It was officially designated for a time as a "swimsuit optional" beach, but the ruling was rescinded later. It still was a nude beach for all who wanted to take the treacherous route down the crumbling cliffs near the University of California's campus at San Diego.

Eyes.

Someone was watching him, concentrating on him with a vigorous and obvious hatred. Like more than half the bathers, Mark wore no swimsuit, and now sat down on his towel on the edge of the dry sand. As casually as possible he surveyed the surrounding naked humanity. Some of the girls were topless only, others nude. A volleyball game was in full swing up the beach. He saw only three people who were seriously overweight.

Just behind a bouncy blonde who had just arrived and was in the process of shedding a two-piece swimsuit, Mark saw the person he decided was generating all of the dangerous vibrations he kept feeling. His first impulse was to walk over and ask her who she was and what she wanted, but he quickly discarded the idea. Instead he would watch the watcher. He slipped into his dry trunks, picked up his towel and, as he shook the sand free, saw the girl clearly: a dark-eyed brunette with waist-length shiny hair and a trim figure, sliding into a coverup kind of light robe. She carried a small towel and a clutch purse as she hurried now to move as he did, but to one side.

During the walk toward the trail, Mark decided two definite types came to Black's Beach: those with good-to-marvelous figures who weren't afraid to brag a little, and the dedicated BAB sunworshippers who were probably also loyal members of a nudist camp in the mountains somewhere.

Mark climbed the first section of the difficult trail quickly, and when out of sight of the brunette took a side trail and crouched behind some overhanging rocks and waited for the girl to move ahead of him on the path.

When she came he saw that she had discarded the towel and her face was cherry red from the exertion. No one else was near them. Again Mark thought of catching up with her and finding out who she was, but he decided it would be a better plan to let her follow him and see what developed. He would rather get the little mystery solved once and for all before he got into his new assignment.

At the top of the trail she stood looking around with growing agitation. Mark walked past without glancing at her and on down a block to where he had parked his rental car, a year-old Pontiac. He pulled out and drove slowly back the way he had come and soon saw a car swing out from its parking place and begin a loose tail. The same brunette was driving. He saw the antenna on the girl's car, and within a half mile another vehicle slid into place behind the girl's, then moved around her and came up close, tailgating Mark's Pontiac, almost bumping his fender.

At once Mark slammed the Pontiac ahead, charging toward the Torrey Pines State Reserve, the rugged, little-used park area between the road and the state beach below the jagged cliffs. He charged past Torrey Pines Municipal Golf Course and soon came to the entrance to the Reserve. A half mile inside the rugged area he jolted to a stop just off the road, bailed out the passenger's side, and darted into a sparsely wooded gully where the torrey pine trees flourished.

The new Oldsmobile came around the last corner cautiously, and skidded to a stop well in back of the Pontiac. Less than half a mile ahead was the park barricade, preventing any further driving in the Reserve.

On his way out of the car, Mark had scooped up his .45 autoloader with the silencer on the nose, and a spare magazine of rounds. Now he peered around a two-foot-thick pine and watched the men in the car. The pair were undecided about what to do, so Mark called the play.

"What the hell kind of game are you guys playing?" Mark called. His voice bounced around the gully until the men were not sure where it came from. Both ducked down in the car, then they slid out the far door. One carried a shotgun, and the other a handgun.

"Over here," Mark said, stepping out from the tree trunk until they saw him, then jolting behind it as both weapons came up. He was well protected a split second before the shotgun thundered and he could hear the double ought buck whacking against the trees and brush. He dropped to his knees and leaned out. Finding the shotgunner aiming another round, the Penetrator blasted off two shots before the scattergun spoke again. The .45 slugs flew straight and true and, despite the slower velocity due to the silencer, slammed into the long-gun man with enough foot-pounds of force to smash him backward. The first slug took him just below the heart, ripping into one lung and lodging there. The second 185-grain chunk of lead penetrated the victim's skull just over his right eye, slanted upward and exploded out the top of his head, removing a three-inch chunk of bone, a mass of brain tissue, and a shower of blood.

His partner, flat on his belly at the side of the road, looked at his dead buddy and screamed. He jumped up, ran forward, his .38 snapping five times, and then a .45 came up in his other hand. Mark waited for him. When he was a dozen paces away, Mark fired, lying on his stomach, leaning around the same tree. He put three rounds into the biggest target area, the gunsel's chest, and he toppled backwards and lay still.

Mark darted to the bodies, pulled out the pockets of their clothing, and on each man found a five-dollar gold piece. He turned them over and on the back were three words in Italian: *Family to Death!* The Mafia password and symbol. He ran to his car and eased it away from the site, turned around fifty feet down the road and drove away. Behind him he heard a siren and then saw a park vehicle skid to a stop next to the Oldsmobile. Mark continued out the park and along the access road to the exit into North Torrey Pines Road.

Mark pulled in at the golf course and parked among the other cars and settled back in the seat. Quickly and automatically he stripped the barrel from the .45 and inserted a new one. He would throw the used barrel in the ocean so there would be no way to trace ballistic reports from the slugs in the Mafia goons to his weapon.

He assembled the weapon again and put a new magazine in the .45, then placed it in the aluminum case that rested on the passenger seat. The Penetrator was reviewing every aspect of his contact so far on his new assignment. There was no chance for a leak on this end. There could have been no possibility of a slip at the Stronghold by the Professor or David Red Eagle. It was then as he had surmised. The dark-haired girl on Black's Beach had recognized him, a chance encounter. There was no way she or anyone else could have known he would go down there today. It had been his impulsive decision. She had made him positively, and when she got to her car she must have radioed or telephoned for reinforcements, then let them take over. That made her Mafia kin, a daughter or a young wife. He did not recognize her. There was more than a good chance that in one of his past missions he had touched her family in some way, and she had remembered him.

Now she knew he was here in the San Diego area. She would find out about her backup men quickly. She probably had the license number of the rental car. He got out of the Pontiac, left the keys on the visor, took his suitcase from the seat beside him, and walked into the clubhouse.

A half hour later he was in a taxi that let him out at a car rental agency in La Jolla. He picked up a new Thunderbird, using his second set of identification the Professor always supplied, and drove down to La Jolla Shores Public Beach and parked. He watched the waves come in as he considered his problem. San Diego had little in the way of organized Mafia. There wasn't enough action to support a family. Various "branch office" teams worked the area from time to time, but there was no indication where the two Mafia soldiers had come from. Their car? He thought back, and for a moment almost had something, but it faded. He let his mind go blank, then pictured the car.

Yes, it was a Nevada license plate. Las Vagas? Sin City had a newly active Mafia family. Maybe they were moving in on the San Diego territory. If so, they would bring in reinforcements quickly and in force. If the girl convinced anyone over there that she had seen the Penetrator, they all would be eager to try for the million-dollar head money that was still outstanding on him. For a million even a Mafia don would expend a little energy.

So now he was well warned.

But he had a job to do, and he better get at it. As long as he wasn't too visible, the creeps would have little chance of finding him. There were one and a half million people in the San Diego area. That's a lot of bodies to look through to find one man.

That decided, he drove on out La Jolla Shores Drive until it came to the campus of the University of California at San Diego, where the San Diego Sharks football team was ensconced for the preseason training camp. He parked at the dorm where the football players would be gathering tonight, with the first report time tomorrow.

For a minute excitement built inside him. He remembered those glory days in high school where a few of the football players were good, and it was a thrill to catch a pass and make a good run. Then college and his UCLA days when he just missed all-American and there had been no pro football draft. He, like most graduating seniors who lettered at college, thought he could make the grade on a pro team, but nobody called.

Now the thought of going out there with pads and helmet and making contact with men ten years younger than he and eighty to 100 pounds heavier sounded like it might not be all that much fun. For a moment he thought about how he used to feel on Sunday after a punishing Saturday college game. Hurt, he hurt all over. In the pros, where every man was a top specialist at his position and had had another ten years of experience in how to create mayhem on a runner without drawing a foul, Mark knew his body was going to be hurting worse than ever before.

But he and the Shark coach, Ben Sample, decided Mark would be a "walk-on" who had enough credits to get a look. Mark couldn't fake it as an assistant coach, but as a walk-on he would live with the players, he would be in on all of the gossip, all the horseplay, and would be able to get to the bottom of this serious injury-on-purpose problem.

Mark had been in town two days. He had spent twelve hours yesterday with Coach Sample going over a special reel of film from the commissioner's office that displayed sixty serious injury accidents last year when players had been hurt, bones broken, knees torn up, and in some cases, suffered serious head damage. They tried to classify the incidents, to categorize them, to show that there was some kind of plan to it all. But the evidence just wasn't good enough.

"What we want you to do, is to get us that

evidence," Coach Sample said. "I've seen it happen, a key player taken out of a game in the first quarter, and the game turns around. You know all of these upsets we've been having? When a damned good team simply gets trampled by a poor team? We think there is a definite plan of some kind. But we're not sure. Now your college coach said you were the man for the job. I don't know who you are, or where you came from. But you say you can play the game well enough to get by for the first two weeks of practice. That should be enough. Those films didn't show it, but last year there were twelve serious injuries in training camps. Twelve and not all of those were accidents. We think most of them were deliberately planned."

Coach Sample was a big man, six-four and 240 pounds. He had been an all-star quarterback six times out of twelve years playing, still had knees he could walk on, and did an outstanding coaching job.

He put one foot on a chair and stared at Mark.

"Son, if you get in too deep, if you want out, you just whistle. You've got my private line. You can call that any time day or night and a beeper will get me in touch within two minutes. We want this mess cleaned up, but I don't aim to see anybody die on account of it."

They shook hands and Mark moved away. Starting today he was just another walk-on, and Coach Sample wouldn't look at him twice, unless he made some outstanding plays.

Mark knew some of the young punks would be faster than he was, but he still had a few moves he could show them. He got out of his car, reminded himself that for the duration he was Pat Wilson, and walked into the dorm to check in and find his room. Festivities got going the next morning at 6 A.M. with breakfast.

2

Big Cully Is Here

An hour after he checked into his room, Mark met his roommate.

"Hi, you've probably heard of me, I'm Cully Ambrose."

Mark nodded. The kid was fresh out of college, six-five, 255 pounds of solid Southern bone and muscle. He went fourth in the first round and the Sharks got him when they traded last year for the first-round pick. He played for Texas, a consensus All-American thought to be a lead-pipe certainty to be a future star as a bruising running back. He was as fast as a scatback and twice as shifty.

Mark held out his hand. "Hi, Pat Wilson, tight end."

Cully looked at him blankly, ignored the hand. "You a veteran? I ain't never heard of you."

Mark laughed. "Thanks, kid. You'll go far, even if you didn't have psychology 104. Are you sure you don't want to be a diplomat?"

"You funnin' with me, old man?"

"Just ease up a little, Cully. You aren't a star yet."

"I wanted to bunk with the quarterback, Fouts."

"Rookies don't bunk with veterans. Take it easy, get your stuff put away, this is going to be a rough two weeks."

Cully dropped on the bed and scowled. "Yeah, tell me about it. Got a buddy who gave me the whole damn schmeer. Kid stuff. I come here to play football, not fuck around with silly-assed pranks."

"It won't last long, Cully, take it in stride or it can get to you and affect your play."

"Hell, nothing but a broken arm will hurt my play."

"You ever had a playing injury, Cully?"

"Hell, no. Played in every game four years at Texas, got more damn minutes than any other offensive player for four years. I play hurt, I ain't no sonofabitching crybaby. You could keep me off the field by breaking my arm, I reckon."

"Sounds reasonable. Now when the veterans start to razz you and give you a bad time, laugh it off the same way you do a bruised shoulder."

Cully watched him, frowning, as he thought about it. "Hey—yah! That makes sense. I'll give it a try. I ain't looking for no fight. I fight the other team."

By 8:30 the next morning breakfast was over and they had met for a half-hour briefing in the gymnasium conference room. There were eighty-two players and some of the veterans hadn't reported in yet. Most were due the next week.

They suited up without pads in shorts and cleats and went out for the first bit of business: time sprints. Mark watched the times, amazed that big men could move so fast from a dead stop. There were times of 4.8 seconds, down to 4.5. And those were the linemen. Some of the defensive backs cut the electronic timer beam at 4.4, along with the wide receivers.

When it was Cully's turn he was all jazzed up. He got in the blocks and came out like a steam engine, but when they read off his time for the 40 yards he had set a mark at 4.3 seconds.

Two of the big tight ends did 4.5's and Mark again was amazed how large these men were, all but him were six-four to six-six. Mark cut the beam at 5.8. He shrugged. Not bad, but still he had some sudden moves they would be surprised at.

Already the assistant coaches were dividing the team into units. Defensive and offensive groups and linemen, receivers, quarterbacks, and defensive backfield. The coaches were getting acquainted with each man, sizing him up in person and checking against scouting reports. There would be run-throughs on the strength machines, and then the physical training would begin. It would be a rugged series of two a day on the field and an evening class on the playbook.

That afternoon Mark saw Cully Ambrose get into a minor shoving match with Ernie Houck, a big defensive lineman. Mark moved in that direction and asked Cully about it.

"That? Nothing. The big sonofabitch told me I'd have fun sitting my ass on the bench all year. I told him the way he played last year he should be on the bench. It was nothing."

Mark scowled and moved away.

That evening they saw the injury film Mark had viewed previously. Coach Sample led it off.

"These are some of the most vicious, outrageous, and criminal kinds of actions I've ever seen on a football field," the coach said. "Nobody loves a good, hard, clean tackle better than I do. But I don't like to see dirty plays, cheap shots, and deliberate attempts to injure, maim, and some-times kill an opponent. That isn't the way we do business, and if I find a player functioning that way he'll be benched and fined and, if it's over the line, he'll be suspended for the rest of the season. It's in the contract. Look at this film for two things: What not to do yourself out there, and what to watch for so it won't happen to you. Roll it."

After the film they broke up into action units for more skull practice and got back to their room just before ten o'clock. Cully turned on a stereo set he had brought and played it until eleven.

Twice Mark suggested he turn it off without results. Ten minutes later Mark got up and pushed the on-off switch and Cully came off his bunk, his fists balled. Mark stood looking slightly up at him.

"Cully, cool it. I'm not as big as you are, but there's a chance I might be a little smarter. I've lived longer, so I damn well better be. You're bright, you know you should have turned it off, so don't get messed up for nothing. You're bigger but I'm faster." Then in a lightning-fast pair of moves, Mark had one of Cully's arms twisted behind his back and another arm around his throat in a choke hold. Before Cully could react Mark released him and stepped away.

Cully pulled his fists up to his hips. "Hownhell you do that?"

"Like I said, Cully, I'm faster than you are. I'd show you, but it took me almost two years to learn it, and we don't have that much time. I'm turning in."

For the first time since he had met Cully, Mark saw him grin.

"Hail! You all right, man! Goddamn, I never seen one human being move so fucking fast in my life!"

"I'd appreciate it if you don't spread it around. It won't do me any good if I don't make the team. I've slowed a step or two so I'm going to have to have glue on my fingers out there."

"Hell, Pat, it's just a game."

Mark laughed. "That, Cully is what the losers always say."

The big running back grinned. "Man, you may be all right. Most of the dudes in this outfit are sassy know-it-alls. Hell, we better get some shut-eye before we got to be up."

He turned off the lights and Mark went to his bed on the other side of the room and thought through his assignment. He didn't have a glimmer yet. Maybe tomorrow.

Mark Hardin was a powerfully built man just

over thirty years old, and carried 205 pounds easily on a broad-shouldered, heavily muscled, six-foot-two-inch frame. He had black hair and eyebrows and dark intelligently glittering eyes. His complexion was a shade darker than white from his Cheyenne blood and he tanned to a coppery brown when he took enough sun. His sharp nose and high cheekbones revealed his half-Cheyenne ancestory. It all gave his face a smoldering, critical expression. When he frowned, a cold, deadly aura came from him.

When moving, Mark had the supple litheness of a young cougar, and the lean, hungry look of a top-condition athlete. He spoke only when it served his purposes, but he could play a role and talk incessantly. His accent was All-American CBS News Neutral, but attentive listeners might detect a slight Far West twang. He tried to make few friends, because all too often a casual acquaintance became a lever to use against him and many times these innocents had died horribly painful deaths.

Now he was on another self-assigned mission. He looked over and saw that Cully went to asleep almost immediately. Good. He was a young, healthy animal. It would take Mark more time.

Another mission. He sighed. Was he getting old-man tired? No. But Mark Hardin knew this one would not be easy. Whenever one person takes on the entire criminal element of American society, he realizes that the odds are against him. But now after fifty-one different attacks on crime, Mark was still functioning and ready to do battle again. Over the years he had grown used to the unthinkable odds, to having the police as well as the hoodlums and killers trying to burn him down. To most police departments, the Penetrator was simply another criminal, because he operated outside the law, functioned as a supervigilante with immediate justice at the end of his deadly .45 autoloader.

In unusual moments of quiet, Mark wondered if he were in a losing battle. His whole life seemed to be a desperate walk on a thin straight edge between legal and criminal, between correctness and corruption, between good and evil. It was easy for Everyman to fall off quickly into the side of crime and never to surface again on the right side.

He had known all of this when he began his crusade, yet he did begin. Mark Hardin is also known as the Penetrator, and he has been battling crime for longer than he wanted to remember.

It all started when hoodlums killed his fiancée and tried to kill him at the same time in a fiery car crash down a ravine near Hollywood. That had launched his one-man attack on crime and he had been doing it ever since. He used dirty money liberated from criminals for his operating bankroll, and the treasury was never empty. Mark had a base of operations he seldom saw anymore, with expert help from Professor Haskins and an ancient Indian, David Red Eagle, who stayed in the Professor's hideaway camouflaged in an old borax mine near Barstow, in the California desert.

More and more the Penetrator had become a

lone warrior, a vengeful hawk, winging down from the sky to blast away at corruption, graft, evil, and menace wherever he found it. He had battled in Japan, Mexico, Canada, France, and Latin America. His targets were manifold but his time limited.

The Penetrator's natural ability as a warrior came from his background. Then, in the Vietnam war, he had taken that native talent and sharpened and honed it into fighting skills with a fine and deadly edge, mastering every hand-held fighting tool the Army could supply him. He became a weapons expert. David Red Eagle had dug into his background and proved him to be half Cheyenne, and had trained him in the quiet, deadly, X-ray-quick ancient Indian fighting methods.

In his fifty-one missions the Penetrator's body had suffered dozens of scars, more than a bullfighter or professional footballer. He had been shot, stabbed, slashed, fractured, crushed, torn, poisoned, and lacerated uncountable times. He knew he was living on a short fuse, walking on cracking ice. He couldn't be lucky forever. One of these days he would be a fraction of an inch too far one way, or move a millisecond too late, and his last mission would end.

Until that last breath came he was a one-man terror of the criminal world—from the huge Mafia syndicates to the international terrorist and crime cartels to the smallest grafter in public office and loan shark shaking down the poor and needy.

Everywhere the corruptors had heard of the

Penetrator and feared him, because they never knew when he might single them out as targets, ending their crime careers and their lives.

And now he was launched on a new effort: to see if there were a conspiracy or a pattern in the debilitating injuries some of the football pros were suffering. Whenever it came to sports, and pro sports especially, there was always the chance of shaving a point spread, of throwing a game, or perhaps even of injuring a player to change the actual *outcome* of a season. None of these elements had been mentioned in his talk with Coach Sample, but they had to be considered. That meant gambling, and the biggest gambling kingpins in the country were involved with sports. So he would strike again.

And he would go on hitting at crime and outlaws and lawbreakers wherever he found them. They all were a cancer on the vitality and the glory of the nation. He had bled for the flag in Vietnam, and he would do so again, any day, putting his life on the line for his country to rid it of these leeches who preyed on the weak and the helpless. He would fight them with every bit of energy and blood that he had left!

For a moment he thought about the two men he had killed today. They had fired at him first, they had proved that they were little better than animals, who ripped and tore and killed and took what they wanted. They were Mafia soldiers, and long ago Mark had promised himself that he would destroy the organized, blood sucking, monster that the Mafia had become. He could best do that by taking down any of the leaders he could find. But until he could get to them, he would strike at any of their soldiers who engaged him in mortal combat.

So today he had again been in a war with the Mafia, on a small scale. He had inflicted casualties on the enemy, it was nothing personal, as the dons were so used to saying, simply business. And two Mafia goons had died. More would take their place, and he would kill them if they came against him.

For now the football problem was paramount, and he must conserve his energy and his abilities to find the pattern, find the inner circle, find the perpetrators of this violence on some of the best players in the league.

He smiled. It had felt good today to be back in the environment of a team situation. His four years of football at UCLA had been a good time for him, had brought him some recognition, though not fame. Now he would be able to relive part of those days, and at the same time find out who had been smashing up the football warriors.

Mark Hardin had his head straight. He turned over and in twenty seconds he was asleep. His mental alarm had been set for five-thirty. He would wake up at that time, automatically.

3

Hit! Hit! Hit!

The next two days were a blur for Mark. They had serious physical training three times a day, they put on pads the third day and began hitting the tackling dummies. It was back to basics that he hadn't thought about since his frosh year in college. Drill, drill, drill.

"Come on you creampuffs, hit that dummy, move that sled, what the hell you think this is, a kindergarten? If you don't want to sweat your balls off you don't belong on this practice field!" That was shouted and echoed over and over again by Coach Sample and the assistant coaches.

Mark found himself running plays, learning the routine. It came back, but slowly. He was in better shape than most of the men in camp. He was always in condition. But many of them were better athletes and he didn't try to compete with them. The Sharks had some all-pro tight ends, and he watched them work out in wonder.

"Wilson, get your tail over here, a down and out. Hit the thirty-yard marker and the ball will be there a yard before you're out of bounds. Move it!"

He jolted out of his stance and made a move inside, then cut to the yard marker and looked back and the ball was in his arms, he cut up field, tiptoed along the side marker for twenty more yards before the safety pushed him over the line.

The offensive coach grunted when Mark came back to the set up where the tight ends and wide receivers were working out. His name was Vuylsteke, and he knew nothing about Mark's real role. He figured to wash out Mark the first week.

"Wilson. We need eighteen yards. Go over the center and get me nineteen. On two."

Mark took a standing position and on the ball snap ran down seven yards, then cut at a forty-five-degree angle across the center to the thirty-five-yard line and looked back, the ball was there, he put it away and made another ten by stutter-stepping a defensive back and again the safety had to tackle him. He protected the ball and held on as he slammed into the turf. At least it was real grass and dirt, not that rock-hard green carpet.

When he came back this time the coach ignored him. Mark got a few curious looks from the other players, then they settled down to another hour of throw and catch before they went back for dummy scrimmage, running through the plays. Everyone in the set was a rookie. The first three exhibition games would be peopled mostly by rookies to see what they could do. Mark hoped he could last until the first game, now less than a week and a half away.

Coach Sample blew his whistle and all motion stopped. "That's it for this morning. Everyone take two laps, and let's remember it's supposed to be a run, not a geriatric convention out there."

In the cafeteria that noon the league's leading pass catcher, wide receiver Lewis Bass, got on Cully.

"Would the gentleman from Texas who was drafted fourth in the first round stand," Bass bellowed.

Mark sat beside Cully and he looked at him. "Better go along with it, can't last long. Let it run off your back," Mark whispered, and slowly Cully rose.

"Well now there he is, southern boy. Hey there Cully, give us a damn rebel yell."

"Never learned how," Cully said.

"Try, son, try," Bass shot back.

Cully gave a screech and sat down quickly. When he did he landed in the middle of his tray of food, which a coconspirator had moved. Cully swore softly and went back to the chow line and picked up a new lunch.

As some of the men finished eating, Bass stood again. "I hear Mr. Cully Ambrose didn't miss a single minute of play in college ball. That so, Cully?"

"Yep."

"Stand, rookie!" Bass shouted.

Cully threw down his spoon and stood. "Damn right, Bass. Not like you did. I ain't no crybaby. I don't drop out 'cause my pinkie hurt. You missed four games last year, I hear."

Bass ignored the jibe. "What would it take to keep you out of a game, hardnose?"

"Broken arm," Cully said and sat down.

Bass gave it up and went out to the practice field.

The afternoon was a repetition of the morning, with Mark starting to feel his body tighten, get the *idea* of being hit and mentally discounting it, jumping up and running back to the huddle.

He also learned as much about the players and rookies as he could, tying down names and numbers and faces, matching them up. He studied the roster as much as the playbook. By the end of the third day he could name eighty per-cent of the players in camp.

Right after the skull session next to the locker rooms, Cully told Mark he was going to take a spin down to the ocean in his car. He had driven to camp in a Cadillac convertible.

"We don't have an ocean like this in West Texas," Cully said. "Gonna jumpa few waves. Come on."

Mark passed, said maybe the next night. He had received a note under the door to call Coach Sample at ten o'clock from a safe phone.

Mark found an enclosed phone booth half a block across campus and dialed the memorized number. The phone rang twice, then someone picked it up.

"Sample here."

"You said to call at ten," Mark said, not otherwise identifying himself.

"Yes, can you talk?" When the coach heard it was safe, he went on. "Why didn't you tell me you could play this game? Hell, if you were about two steps faster you could make this team. Damn fine showing. But you'll be cut. Anything new?"

"Nothing. Not enough veterans in camp yet. I know most of the rookies and walk-ons. I have to make the first cut, when is it, this Saturday?"

"Right. I've got the fix in for you for one more week. I may have to tell one or two coaches, so they won't make you look too slow."

"You know where something like these deliberate injuries lead, Coach?"

"Damn right, point spread shaving, maybe a key man or two faking an injury. We both know it comes down to the gamblers, but neither of us is going to mention it. I want this cleaned up before the regular season starts, even if it costs me two starters."

"Two starters?"

"I've been hearing things. Something about an organization. That's all I know. The idea is that two men from each team are in some kind of a group. It wouldn't be my quarterback or my big fullback. Anybody else is expendable to get something like this straightened out. Now get it moving, man. We need results."

"Right. Something should surface soon. More and more of the veterans are back. We wait and we watch. Any injuries yet beside pulled muscles?

"A knee, but he did it exercising. Besides, that one is fifty pounds overweight."

"Right. I better get back. I'll stay in touch."

Mark hung up and walked to the dormitory. Cully wasn't there. Mark studied his playbook for half an hour, memorized all the plays and the call names and snap numbers that he could be involved with. He stopped when he heard the siren wail outside.

An ambulance whined to a stop near the team doctor's office and somebody got out of the ambulance. In the light, Mark identified the man . . . . Cully. It took Mark two minutes to get to the team physician's office where they had just put Cully into the portable X-ray unit. When the pictures came out of the soup they knew it was a fracture of both bones in Cully's right arm.

By that time Coach Sample was in the office. He stormed up one side and around the table and roared at Cully.

"Well, don't just sit there like a damn Texas asshole! Tell us what happened!"

Cully's eyes were wary. "I went down to the beach to jump a few waves, and on the way back I had a little crash. Guess I wasn't watching the road. Didn't hurt the car much, but. . . ."

"I don't care about the goddamned car, Cully. You're prime beef. You're first round. What the hell do we tell the press about how the fuck you broke your arm?" He spun around. "Doc, how long, Doc? He be out for eight, nine weeks?"

"Nine or ten," Dr. Zeiss said. "It's a bad break, Ben."

Coach Sample whirled around and glared at

Cully. "Why didn't you take your roommate with you? You know I don't like you guys charging around here. Who is your roommate?"

Cully pointed at Mark. Coach Sample spun around. "Who are you?"

"Wilson, coach."

"Next time, Wilson, you're assigned a first-round draft pick, you take better care of him." Coach Sample stormed around the room, then stopped in front of the doctor. "Well, Zeiss, for Christ's sakes, get the arm set so it can start healing. Put a good cast on it, and no pins, you hear? I don't want any damned infection from those dirty pins you always use."

Coach started for the door, then turned back to Mark. "You, Wilson. You stick with Cully like goddamned glue until he's safely in his beddy-bye, is that clear?"

Mark nodded and the coach stormed out. Dr. Zeiss cleared everyone out except Mark and then studied the X-rays. He put Cully's arm under a fluoroscope and pulled Cully's hand and turned the arm slightly. Mark looked in the scope and saw the break and how the bones had now been worked back into position again.

Sweat beaded Cully's forehead, and Dr. Zeiss nodded.

"Most players scream for ten minutes when I do that," Dr. Zeiss said. "You're a tough one."

An hour later Cully lay on his own bed, his forearm wrapped and cast solidly from fingers to elbow and in a sling around his neck.

Mark closed the door after brushing the last of the curious out of the room. Then he turned a chair around and leaned on the back as he stared at Cully.

"Damned unusual to break an arm in a minor car crash," Mark said.

Cully looked up. There was fury in his eyes that hadn't been there before. "Christ, but I'm glad to get alone with you, Wilson. You got to help me. I didn't break my arm in the car crash. Some goons ran me off the road, grabbed me and before I figured out what they were doing, one sonofabitch broke my arm over his knee like a piece of kindling. Then they got in their car and burned rubber getting away. I stood there for an hour before anyone would stop and call the cops."

"Yeah, that makes more sense. Goons? What do you mean?"

"Big guys, dumb as dirt, both of them had shoulder holsters with guns in them. One talked with a New York accent, heavy. Both Italian looking. Hell, they could have stepped right out of The Godfather."

"They weren't football players?"

"Hell, no. Big, dumb, Italian."

"What kind of a car were they driving?"

"Black Cadillac sedan. Big job."

"What kind of license plate?"

"License plate. Yeah, I saw it when I got out. Not California, I saw that when I jumped out. Yeah, white letters on a blue background."

"Nevada?"

"Could have been."

"Cully, I'd say you got on somebody's nerves. Somebody doesn't want you around camp any more, or they don't want you to play football for the Sharks this year. All we have to do is find out which, and who they are."

Cully looked up at him. "You're more than a football player, right, Wilson? You from the commissioner's office or something? Damn but that arm hurts! I can tell you one thing for sure: I ain't going to leave camp. I'll stay right here and learn the plays and keep in good condition, run a lot. I'll be ready to play when this wing gets healed."

"Hey, Cully, I'm not from the commissioner's office. I don't know what you're talking about. I'm just an old war horse who had a connection and got to come out and scrimmage with the pros for a week or two. Damn big thrill for me even though I know there is no way I can make the squad. But I don't like to see people like you pushed around."

"Yeah, whatever. But what the hell do I do now? I can't play, so I watch. I can't even work a clipboard, the bastards broke my right arm." He slammed his open palm against the wall. "Damnit! You told me to take it easy that first day. I guess I didn't. I shoot off my mouth sometimes."

"A first-round man has a lot of people out there who want to take a shot at him, to see if they are as good as you are. But this broken arm thing is different. That was what you said in the cafeteria this noon that it would take to get you out of the game. Now you cool it. You've still got a contract, you'll get paid. They'll put you on injured reserve, and you probably won't travel with the team, but don't sweat it."

Cully nodded, pulled off his clothes, and slid into bed.

Mark undressed and went to bed as well, and went to sleep after asking himself a few questions. Two goons: Nevada plates. That should mean Mafia. Someone on the team had good enough connections to get a pair of torpedoes to break a star's arm. That was a solid connection. Mark hoped the same man didn't come in contact with the Mafia female type with the long black hair. No way. But still he wondered about it. Lewis Bass was the big loser in the shouting match with Cully. Tomorrow Mark might pay a quick visit to his room to check it out. So far he was the only suspect, and a poor one. If Bass were the man with the Mafia connection, he wouldn't let it be so plain for everyone to see. Bass was not the man. That left a dozen or more veterans already in camp.

Someone shook the doorknob. Mark sat upright. In the dim light he saw a white envelope pushed under the door. He jolted to the panel, jerked it open, but there was no one in the lighted hallway. Mark closed the door and locked it, then picked up the envelope. Inside was a three-by-five card. On it in red letters were the words: "Wilson we don't like you either. You have two days to quit camp and stay in one piece. After that you go out feet first."

4

First Rise to Bait

When the Penetrator woke up at 5 A.M. as planned, he was still glad that someone had sent him the threatening note under his door. It showed there were some creeps in the team camp, and that his little charade hadn't fooled everyone. Or it could be that the note was a shot in the dark. He was a little out of his element among all of these "trees." It also meant he could make himself a target and get one notch up the goon's chain of command by nailing the attacker.

He dressed quickly, jogged to his favorite phone booth and called the coach. The phone rang only once.

"Yeah?"

"Coach Sample, you asked me to call you. Cully did not break his arm in the car crash. Two goons forced his car off the road. When he got out they jumped him and one broke Cully's arm over his leg like a piece of kindling. Last night someone sent a threatening note to me under my door. Things are starting to move."

"Shit! Somebody broke it!"

"True, Coach. Cully wants to stay in camp. He's worth it. I'd keep him here. I'll wait and see if anybody makes a move on me. I'd say our heavies have to be one or two of the twelve veteran players you have in camp right now."

"Figures, but I can't pick them out. Shit! Why can't we just play football?"

"We will, coach. Don't tell Cully I told you this or he'd know I was a ringer. He could use some cheering up today, though."

"Right, I'll have him in for a talk." The coach paused. "You always get up this early?"

"When I'm working, coach."

"Yeah, right. Be careful."

The line went dead and Mark jogged back to his room and got in just as Cully woke.

Nothing happened at breakfast.

When Mark got to his locker to suit up for calisthenics, he found the lock pried off and all his gear soaked with motor oil. They had even left the can. He carried the whole mess to the equipment room, where the manager screamed at him for ten minutes while he issued him new gear.

Back in the locker room a big tackle eased past him.

"Somebody don't like your ass, man," the huge black man said.

"I ain't in no popularity contest," Mark said. "All I got to do is bust asses."

The man turned and grinned. "Right on!" he said and jogged outside.

At the practice Cully was on the sidelines. He wore his shorts and Shark jersey and a sling. He did all the exercises that he could and worked hard on the running, usually leading the pack even with his broken arm.

In one drill when Mark had some free moments Cully came over and they talked.

"Brothers," Cully said softly. "That's a term I've heard a few times. It's spoken in whispers and from friend to friend. The idea I get is that the Brothers are some kind of enforcers, some superspooks who keep everyone in line. Hell, I don't know anything more. Maybe the Brothers had my arm broken. I get mostly blank stares when I ask the veterans about them."

Mark tried the same tactic. The big tackle Sparky Monroe, who had talked to Mark in the locker room, froze when he mentioned the term. Monroe shook his head and walked away.

In a scrimmage that afternoon, Mark was blocking on a sweep right, had bounced off a charging All-Star defensive end, and was out of the play when he sensed someone hurtling down on him. He jolted to one side suddenly, and Monroe brushed past him in a slashing late hit.

Sparky Monroe was a backup veteran tackle who did a lot of bench time, but played behind two great tackles. He was good and he knew better than to pull a late hit on his own teammates.

Mark rolled over and jammed his hand onto

Monroe's facemask and pinned his head to the ground.

"What the hell you doing, Monroe? You blind-sided me about an hour after the play was over."

Big brown eyes rolled and looked up at him. "What? Over? Christ. Hey, man. Take it cool. I had a couple of joints this noon and my timing is still off. Accident. Okay?"

Mark rolled over and came to his feet.

"Accident, hell, Sparky. You just tried and missed. You better not try again or you'll be the one with a broken arm."

"It was just the damn pot. . . ."

"Save that for somebody who'll believe you, like the Brothers."

Sparky was on his feet at once, his fist balled, but then he relaxed slowly and walked back to the huddle.

Mark watched out for himself during the rest of the scrimmage, and came out without getting killed, but took a few solid shots that were not necessary. He gave back just as good as he got, once smashing Sparky down from the side in a crushing block that left Sparky wincing as he got up. He glared at Mark, but didn't have a chance to return the favor.

That night, While Cully slept, Mark found Sparky's room and went to it, picked the lock and slipped inside silently. Sparky had been assigned a veteran roommate, but the lineman hadn't reported to camp yet. He was due next week.

Mark locked the door, but a chair under the knob, and snapped on the overhead light. The room was bigger than Mark's and Sparky came up from his bed blinking and swearing.

"What the fuck? . . ."

"You and I are going to have a little heart-to-heart, Sparky. Wilson is the name if your contact lenses aren't in, and I want to know exactly *why* you tried to clobber me today and *who* told you to do me in."

Sparky stared at Mark for a minute, then started to laugh.

"Why don't you just be smart, old man, and fade out of camp. Nobody wants you here. Hell, you can play ball, but no way are you gonna make the team. The rookies don't know, but the veterans had you figured for a ringer the first two days of camp. Now get your ass out of here and you won't get busted up none."

"There's nobody in camp who can bust me up, black man."

Sparky jumped off the bed. He was six-eight and weighed two hundred and eighty-five pounds. "How about me, honkey? Then if you get lucky and put me away, there's a dozen lined up behind me to take their turn. You gonna put us all away?"

Before Sparky had the last word out of his mouth, Mark did a spinning back kick, snapping his body around with all his weight behind it, and his sneaker heel landed solidly just below Sparky's rib cage and slightly on the back of his right side, directly over his kidney. The blow jolted Sparky to one side, then the effects of the kidney blow hit him and he doubled up on the floor, pulling up his legs in agony.

He turned to one side and vomited, then hugged his knees. For three minutes he couldn't talk, then he exploded with a gush of swearing. Monroe gasped between each word, and at last had the pain and the bile enough under control.

"You son of a bitch! You cheap-shot artist! You sneaky bastard!"

Mark toed Sparky's chin upward and stared at him. "Monroe, let's talk about the Brotherhood. Who told you to pour the oil on my gear? Who told you to push the note under my door? Who told you to take that cheap blindside at me today?"

"Go fuck yourself, Wilson."

Mark's toe tapped the kidney area again and Sparky screamed.

"When I get up from here, I'm gonna kill you, Wilson!"

"Not without some help. Now, do you talk or do I use some karate on you and tear off one of your ears?"

The black man sagged. He held up a plate-sized hand spread in supplication. "Hell, man. You know I can't tell you any of that stuff. I'm the bottom of the line. I just get a nod or a whisper and then I go and do it. I don't know who's up the line. And I need the bread, know what I mean? Coke is getting more expensive, and I'm into that a little. Hell, man, you can't expect me to give you no names. I wouldn't know who the Brothers were if you told me. Got my guesses, and I know for damn sure not all of them on all the teams are black. Hear they're called the Brothers of Blood. But that's it. I just do what I'm told, man, nothing less, nothing more."

Mark dropped in front of the big player and, so quickly there was no defense, clapped both his palms toward each other with Sparky's head and ears in between. He used medium force, not wanting to deafen the big man. But it was plenty to send shock waves of ringing pain through Sparky's ears and a grinding pain through his head. Quickly Mark slapped Sparky's face back and forth with three blows on each side. Sparky wailed in anger and pain and sprawled full length on the floor.

Mark sat in a chair opposite him, alert, watchful of a charge, and waited watching Sparky recover his hearing and get control of himself.

"Who the hell *are* you?" Sparky asked at last.

"I'm a friend of a guy you had beat up and his arm broken, and I don't like that, Sparky. Now who's the next man up the line? I want a name and it better be the right one, or your ass is heading for the waiver list with one hell of a big blast of bad publicity about your coke habit and your enforcer role on the Shark squad. It will be plenty to finish you in football. Are you listening to me, asshole?"

The big face came up and there were tears on Sparky's cheeks.

"Hey, man, not that. No blackball. No way. Hey, I can't do nothing else but play ball. I'd be on welfare inside of two months. Give me a break, man. Come on. I give you the name but you don't no way let on how you know. You got to protect me from him or I'm one dead nigger. How about that?"

Mark nodded. "Who is it?"

"Hey, man. You got to swear you won't bring me into it. I don't even know you, never talked to you, right?"

Slowly, Mark nodded.

"Christ, I could wind up dead. Hell, at least I'll have a fucking *chance* to play another season. His name is Dabrowski, Vic Dabrowski, first-string pulling guard and a damn good one."

"You swear he's the one who gives you assignments?"

"Christ, yes! You think I'd lie to you now?"

Mark eased off the chair, turned and pushed the chair toward the big man, who had lifted to his knees and began to dive for Mark as soon as he turned his back. Monroe tried to catch the chair, but it made a gash an inch long over his left eye.

Mark removed the other chair from under the door handle and unlocked it. "Nice try, Sparky, but no rubber duck. You better not have lied to me about Dabrowski."

There was nothing Mark could do that night. He went back to his third-floor room and looked down at the courtyard below. Dabrowski, it might be another step up the line. This thing seemed to be set up with as much protection between the soldiers and the actual Brothers as the Mafia had between their soldiers and their dons.

He slid into his room, locked the door and got into bed. Cully was snoring softly across the room.

It was a damn shame the Mafia had been brought into this. So the kid mouthed off a little, he was young. But it had only reinforced the Penetrator's beliefs. Somebody had to stand up against the bastards in society. There were only two types of people, the takers and the givers. The takers swarmed all over others, using them, taking from anyone what they wanted, riding roughshod over the wants, desires, and the rights of everyone else.

On the other hand there were the givers, who helped out their fellow man, stood up to the takers and made them back down, and contributed something to the general welfare of the human race.

There were too few of the givers.

Right now Mark wanted to be one of the takers: to ride over the Mafia, to trample into extinction this Brotherhood of Blood. To rattle the cages of fifty-six professional football players who had set themselves up as minigods to impose their will or that of their directors on the sport of football . . . and do it all for profit, for dirty money profit through fixed gambling odds and results.

Not often did Mark think back. He had sustained fifty-one missions fighting crime and evil and corruption wherever he found it. Now he was on another assignment. He would keep on fighting and protesting and waging his vigilante war with the underworld and the detested Mafia for as long as he could, for as long as his mind and body held together so he could investigate a situation and could pull a trigger. He didn't care if the corrupt blood of hoodlums splattered him, stained him, gave him a criminal reputation with some and that of a modern Robin Hood with others. It was his task in life and he would follow it through.

What angered him here was the ability of a few men to control an entire football league of twenty-eight teams that affected millions of fans. To be able to pull the strings that might make a team win or lose. Mark wasn't worried about the gambling—gamblers were a strange breed who would always be around, and who by their very nature were suckers for the criminal element to cheat and manipulate. But what he did hate was the idea that young men like Cully and other players could be smashed down, and their lives affected, their careers ruined, and in some cases their very lives be snuffed out, all because some manipulator somewhere decided that it should happen to make him a few dollars!

That manipulator was the man Mark wanted!

That was the bastard he would ferret out and smash into eternity before this mission was concluded!

5

Swim or Sink

All the next day, Mark waited for something to happen, some confrontation, a blackjack along-side his head, something.

Nothing did.

Just after dinner, Cully talked him into riding with him to the beach. They could go down to La Jolla Shores and jump a few waves. He had a watertight wrap put on the cast so it wouldn't get wet and the team physician said it would be all right.

Mark remembered the last time Cully went off campus alone, so he tagged along, but took a few minor tools of his trade with him. There is no place on a swimsuit to hide a .45, so he left it behind.

It was still two hours until sunset when they ran into the breakers and swam. Cully launched into a flutter kick backstroke just inside the breaker line. They clowned for half an hour, then went back to their towels.

They heard a kid shouting something down the beach and as he came closer Cully sat up and listened.

"Hey, you hear that? The kid said somebody left on his car lights, and then he gave my license plate number. I didn't even *have* my lights on."

"You stay here, I'll go look," Mark said. The other shoe had dropped. Somebody wanted them in the parking lot or wanted to separate them. It would be better to stay together. He told Cully to come and bring the stuff. Mark wished he'd brought along a weapon; even Ava would come in handy.

They went into the lot casually, half a block from where they had parked and worked toward it as if lost. Mark took a four-inch throwing knife from the side of his swimsuit and now carried it in his palm with the blade along his wrist and out of sight.

Mark moved slightly ahead. The Caddy sat where they had left it, no punctured tires, no broken windows. They leaned on another car as if waiting for the man with the keys to come. Mark saw movement just beyond the Cadillac. He dropped the pose and walked that way. There was a chance the visitors didn't get a good look at him when they came. Cully would be a fast make with his broken arm in a cast. Mark went through the line quickly and came up behind a man in a suit squatting between cars. He was staring over a fender at the Caddy. Mark moved up silently behind him, saw the .45 in his right hand by his side. Mark pushed the sharp point of the blade against the man's neck and grabbed the .45 at the same time.

"Damned strange place to take a leak," Mark said. The man powered backward, the knife penetrating an inch before Mark jerked it free. Mark clubbed the .45 from the man's hand and he fell flat on his back on the macadam. He had the suit, the .45, and the inept snarl of a Mafia soldier.

"Where the hell you come from?" the goon asked.

"Where you weren't looking. Where's your backup?"

"No backup. I'm alone."

"Fat chance. Push under this car with your feet and leave just your head and shoulders out." The hood did as he was told. A moment later Mark heard a snarl behind him and turned to see a man with a .45 sighting in. Mark snapped a shot from the gift .45 and dove forward to the paving, then rolled toward the car and fired again.

The second round split the Mafia goon's nose and blasted upward into his skull, reducing by one the number of enemy Mark faced.

When he turned, the man under the car was getting up. Mark threw the knife and saw the four-inch blade drive straight into the soldier's spinal column. He took two more steps and dissolved onto the pavement. The shots had attracted attention. Mark wiped his prints off the .45 and threw it under a car. Staying low, he worked to the far side of the parking lot and reappeared, walking around the end of the lot, calling for Cully. The running back saw him and joined him as they worked back to the beach.

"Two of them were waiting, and you can bet there's at least two more in here somewhere as backup. Mafia types you saw before. We better take a swim."

Mark looked at the parking lot as they walked and soon saw two men in suits and hats moving through the cars. They were angling toward the water in the same direction Mark and Cully were walking.

"Getting wet time," Mark said. He dropped the towel Cully had given him. "We move into the water and straight out to sea." There's a pier about a quarter of a mile down. Can you swim a 440?"

"I was on the swim team at Texas. I can do a quarter of a mile with no hands. I've got an especially bouyant body."

By then they were running into the waves and Mark saw the two gunsels running for the wet sand. Both swimmers were fifty yards out by the time the hunters came to the water. Mark and Cully ducked under the last breaker and they were beyond the line. Mark pointed north and they swam for the line of pilings. It was the Scripps Institution of Oceanography pier, and not at all public, but any port in a storm would do. No matter where else they beached, the goons would be there with plenty of hot lead waiting for them.

Mark looked over and saw that Cully was five yards ahead of him, doing a variation of the breast stroke with one arm, and making good time. Mark put his face in the water and did three double strokes, then looked up. They were still a long way from the pier. Cully didn't seem to tire. They stroked for another five minutes, then Mark called for him to tread water a minute. Mark checked the shore, but nowhere could he spot the two men in suits. They both floated for a while, and Cully kept making wild remarks, and suddenly Mark wondered if Cully knew more about this whole situation than he was saying.

They stopped twice more before they came to a ladder on the pier and a pretty blonde girl who shouted at them that they couldn't climb up.

Mark ignored her until he was up the ladder and helping Cully. Going up a ladder with one hand is a tricky operation. When she saw the cast the girl stopped shouting at them and helped get Cully to the platform.

She was tiny and blonde and wearing a one-piece swimsuit that explained completely how she was constructed. Her blue eyes led a smile as she put her hands on shapely hips.

"So. Explanations, please."

Mark took it straight. "We'd like you to call the San Diego Police. We were on the beach and two men with guns started running toward us and we swam out, but the men wouldn't leave, so we came down here where they couldn't follow us."

The girl frowned. "For real?"

"For real, Miss," Cully said and a generous portion of his Texas drawl came through. She looked at him more closely.

"You're from Texas?"

"Yes, indeed, pretty lady."

"And you have a broken arm, and you're big enough and about twenty-one. You must be Cully Ambrose."

"Why, yes, I am."

"Sorry about your arm. I read about you in the paper. Just wait until next year."

She smiled at Cully as she lifted a phone from a wall mount and spoke briefly. When she hung up, she smiled.

"You have a car in the La Jolla Shores parking lot?"

"Yes, ma'am."

"Two of our armed security guards will meet us at the end of the pier and take you both back to your car and then escort you back to UCSD. You're both in Shark camp there, right?"

Cully nodded.

She walked beside Cully all the way down the pier to shore and then kissed his cheek goodbye. The security guards looked competent. Cully assured them he had his key, and they got in the back of the Ford and sat on dry towels the girl had magically provided.

"You come back and see me," she said smiling at Cully. "My name is Marsha, Marsha Day."

"I'll do that, Marsha," Cully said, and they drove away.

Mark checked out the Cadillac. There were fifteen policemen around. A coroner's van was there as well as an ambulance. The area was roped off and they were letting cars out one at a time. Mark took the Caddy's key and went up to the spot and ten minutes later was back with the Cadillac.

"Trouble?" Cully asked.

"Just a little."

"Those shots we heard when we were here before?"

"True, Cully. A couple of dudes seemed to have shot up each other. Glad we got away in time."

They drove the long way home. Mark went out Ardath Road, up U.S. Highway 5 and back on La Jolla Village Drive to the university.

"This way, Cully, nobody surprises us on the way back to the campus. Somebody out there just don't like us."

"Yeah. I been meaning to talk to you about that. You hear any more about this Brotherhood?"

"A little, but don't worry about it."

"I'm not worrying, old man, just wondering. I've heard they are some kind of enforcers. But what the hell do they enforce?"

Mark parked the Caddy, gave Cully the keys and they went up to their room. Mark hadn't had time to think much about the Brotherhood contact name he'd been given, Vic Dabrowski. One of the best pulling guards in the league. He could fake a block and get out in front of a runner on a sweep before the tackles knew what was happening.

How far up the ladder was Dabrowski?

After twenty minutes of searching, Mark found Dabrowski shooting pool in the recreation room. He was good. He was playing eight ball for five dollars a ball left on the table. He broke on the next game, pocketed a two ball and cleaned off his solid balls, and then sank the eight ball without giving the rookie wide receiver a shot. He asked for a challenger and Mark went down. Mark flipped him and won the break and had three stripes down before Dabrowski got a shot. Mark won the game with one of Dabrowski's solids on the table. The big guard gave Mark a five-dollar bill and demanded a rematch. This time it was loser shoots first and Dabrowski won with two of Mark's balls up. Mark paid him the ten and sat back and watched. Dabrowski was quick and sharp mentally, he probably even graduated from the college where he majored in football. He would be a man worth watching. But he wasn't stupid. Mark would need some kind of a lever to get anything more than a roaring denial out of Dabrowski.

Mark left the recreation room and went out to the exterior steps that led to the third-floor rooms. The stairs were covered but "arty" according to one brand of architecure. He had just started up the first flight when he heard yelling above. Mark leaned out and looked up and saw two people struggling with each other at the third-level railing. Then someone screamed and Mark leaned back in as a body fell past him and hit the cement sidewalk below. Mark rushed down the three steps to the sidewalk.

The huddled, broken body had landed on its side and crumpled, one leg askew, the torso compressed and one arm extending at a grotesque angle. *The arm was in a cast!*

The Penetrator rushed forward and bent low. It was Cully, and he barely clung to life. His bloodied face moved, his eyes opened and he gasped. Then he said one word, "Brotherhood," before he died.

The Penetrator raced up the steps to the third floor. Two rookies leaned over the rail, staring below. Mark grabbed them.

"Did you see it happen? Did you see Cully go over the railing?"

"It was Cully?" one asked. "My God. I just got here." The other player said he just ran up as well. No one had come down the steps. But there were stairs at the other end of the building. The Penetrator ran through the third floor hallway to the stairway at the other end and rushed down the steps. No one lurked there on any of the landings. Someone could have stepped into a room on either the second or third floor. There would be no way to find him now.

An ambulance growled up outside and by the time Mark walked back the campus police had cordoned off the area and were keeping everyone back.

Mark stared at Cully's body. What a waste, what a tragedy! What a murder. Why Cully? Had they been aiming at Mark instead? Did someone think Cully was Wilson? It wasn't likely. Mark walked to the phone he always used and dialed the coach's number. He was in session with his assistants. Mark told him what happened in one sentence.

"I'll be right there. The newspapers are going to have a field day with this one. Say nothing about a struggle. He must have got dizzy and fallen."

Mark hung up the phone. It was starting again. The takers were moving in. They were exacting their price. But why Cully? Why was he singled out, of all the rookies? Not because he had a big mouth. This was something else, something he almost talked about today but not quite. Mark knew he had to have another long conversation with Coach Sample.

It was almost 1:30 A.M. before the police left, the curious melted away, and Mark and Coach Sample met in the darkness between the walkway lights and the street lamps.

"It was murder, Coach, deliberate, planned murder. I don't know if I can stay under cover much longer. I don't know if it will do any good."

6

Little Miss Angie—For Real

Coach Ben Sample's mouth was tight, his expression grim. Mark knew he had called the commissioner, getting him out of bed at four in the morning eastern time. The coach walked around in a small circle as Mark had seen him do on the sidelines during close games. He came back and stared at Mark.

"Wilson, right now, I *need* you. You're all we've got left. I didn't even know it, but Cully Ambrose was working directly with the commissioner's office to try to break this injury thing. The Commissioner got a whiff of it late last year and he's been digging all summer with no result. He asked Cully if he'd take a swing at it in camp and he said sure. Cully was a good lad, Wilson, and would have been a running back to make everyone forget about Jim Brown. But not now. Right now you're all I've got. I told the commissioner what we're doing. He gave us his blessing, and some more facts. You were right. The group is called the Brotherhood of Blood and they have two members in each of the twenty-eight teams. They take orders from someone, and that's the big fish we need. If we chop off the head of this group, we think we will cut the money supply at the same time, and the Brotherhood will die out almost overnight."

Mark thought about it. At last he nodded. "Some of the veterans know that I'm not good enough to make the team. One or two already think I'm a ringer. How about tomorrow I pull a hamstring and be on the disabled bench for a while. I'll still be inside, still have access to everyone, but I won't have to perform good enough to stay on the squad."

Coach Sample nodded. "Good. And I'm bringing in my own security. I'll have four men on duty around the clock. Somebody out there killed once, they could do it again." He frowned. "Heard about a little fracas down at the beach late this afternoon. You and Cully?"

"Yes. Two guys who could only be Mafia goons tried to burn us down. I didn't want that to happen, so both of them cashed in their chips. I don't figure you want to hear about it. That's one we don't have to tell the police about. Believe me, both those dudes deserved whatever they got."

Coach Sample stared at Mark. "I don't know much about you, Wilson. But my source says you work only for the good guys. I guess I'll have to take that as gospel. But I do know for damn certain that I don't want any more of my people hurt. And I don't want the team or any of us involved in any illegal actions. If it happens, just be damn certain you're not tied to it." He paused and made another one of his nervous little circle walks. When he came back to Mark he shook his head.

"I didn't bargain for Cully getting killed when he came into camp. I thought he was the future of the franchise. Now he's dead and it's partly my fault. I *did* bring you in, and I don't want to bend over and look at your cold, stiff form, too. You make goddamned sure that you don't get yourself killed."

Mark thought he saw a trace of tears at the corner of Coach Sample's eye as he turned and walked quickly across campus to his car.

Mark leaned against a tree watching the police take down the last of the yellow tape that sealed off the death scene. When the downstairs cops were gone, Mark knew there would still be detectives in the room. He knew it would be sealed too, so he went to his rented car in the parking lot and sat in the back seat and went to sleep. It wouldn't be long until dawn, and then he had more work to do.

Less than four miles away in a La Jolla condominium, someone else could not sleep. Her name was Angie Lavangetti, and she was the same delicious, long-haired brunette Mark had seen nude on Black's Beach a few days before. She sat looking at the picture of Cully Ambrose from yesterday's *Tribune*, and she was positive. She had trailed along with four men that afternoon to La Jolla Shores Beach to see that they did their work properly. It was a simple hit on an overzealous football player. It would have been routine, only the mark brought a friend along.

Then the friend got tricky, and two of her soldiers were in the county morgue and two more were getting their asses chewed for not doing their job.

She had moved in when she heard the gunfire, and remained on the sidelines, but she got a good look at Cully with his broken arm and the other man, the same tall dark one she had seen on Black's Beach. . . . the Penetrator! From the way he put down her two men so quickly she was sure now it was him. She had called Vegas and they were sending over a crew wagon with six good men. Soon, very soon, they would collect the head money offered for the Penetrator!

She sat on the edge of the bed in the darkness, walked to the picture window and opened the drapes so she could look out on the jewel lights of La Jolla. Breathtaking, after the desert dryness of Las Vegas. She slipped off her thin robe and slid into the bed nude. It was the only way to sleep. And she would celebrate again by going to Black's Beach, just as soon as she had the Penetrator's head in a plastic sack.

She rolled over and one hand touched her breast. She wondered what it would be like with a man like the Penetrator? Wild? Fast? No, he would be slow and tender, thoughtful, and then try to kill her as he climaxed. She smiled. No, she wasn't thinking about the Penetrator. That's the way *she* would do it to him if she ever had the Penetrator in her power. Her hand rubbed one breast again, then the other one. Her dark eyes glistened as she reached for the telephone and dialed. It rang four times before a sleepy male voice answered.

"Good morning. Do you know who this is?"

There was a soft chuckle. "Yes."

"Good, get over here. Use your key at the back gate. You be here in ten minutes or your ass is in a sling."

"I'll be there."

She put down the phone, closed the drapes and put on some soft music. Then she turned on one dim light in the living room and one in her bedroom and uncorked a bottle of champagne. The celebration might be a little premature, but this way she could have two celebrations. Two. She thought about it. It had been a long time since she had played with two men at once. That would be the real celebration when she had the Penetrator's head. It would be easy now. He had been with Cully. So he was either a player, coach, or somehow connected to the San Diego Sharks. Now that she had him pinned down that close by, it would be simple. Especially since tomorrow was the first day they let the public in to watch the Shark workouts at UCSD.

Angie smiled. It was going to be a fine month in San Diego after all, not at all the dull stay she had expected.

Angie giggled and sipped the champagne. It wasn't pink but it would do until her little friend got there.

*   *   *

By the time Mark crawled out of his car and staggered into the cafeteria used exclusively by the Shark's football camp people, there were a dozen newspeople buttonholing everyone. A half hour later the TV trucks and their minicameras swarmed in from the local stations, Los Angeles, and the networks. Everyone wanted to talk to everyone. Mark shied away from any kind of an interview, and cut a half block around any TV crew.

Mark listened to the questions. Disbelieving ones that betrayed a strong suspicion that something was wrong here.

"Was Cully a drug user?" one woman sportswriter asked. "Wasn't he known to smoke a reefer and snort cocaine now and then? Could he have been high on something, and have simply tripped and fallen off the balcony?"

The team publicist stormed up and took over, demanding that such cynical speculation not be aired until after the autopsy and a complete evaluation of body tissue had been done.

"I'm positive that the coroner's report will show that there were no drugs in Cully's system with the exception of the pain medicine prescribed for him. That was extra-strength aspirin."

"But how could a peak-condition athlete fall off a balcony?" the woman persisted. "Was he having a bad time with the veterans? Was the rookie syndrome getting to him, especially since he was drafted so high?"

"No," one of the players said. "Cully got along fine with everyone. Sure, he took his share of ribbing, nothing serious, and nothing that got out of hand."

"Is the report true about how he broke his arm?" the same reporter asked.

One of the tackles who stood six-six and weighed in at 274 pounds walked up to her and glared down. "Lady, you sure you on the right job? This is a football team, not the Watergate team. You want to dig up dirt, you go look how the welfare cheats are ripping off us working folks. You just leave Cully alone. The boy is dead, let him rest in peace. You're the kind of reporters that good TV stations don't need."

"Thank you, and what's your name?" she asked.

"What the hell is your name, lady reporter?" he shot back.

"I'm Carla Furman, Channel Six."

"See, I knew you could get one fucking thing right." The big tackle turned and stomped away, leaving a red-faced reporter.

An hour later they were still there, swarming over the practice field, getting in everyone's way. So far the team had been able to do exactly nothing, not even do their warmup exercises. At last Ben Sample got on a bull horn.

"Now hear this. You newspaper, TV, and radio reporters have twenty minutes more, then this is going to be a closed practice, and everyone without specific permission must be off the field. To encourage you, our defensive line will remove anyone trying to stay late. We don't call them the Devastators for nothing."

There were some laughs, but they were all gone on schedule.

As the last of the newspeople left, Mark saw a familiar figure and face. It was the small blonde from the Scripps pier. He ran over to the gate and called to her. She turned and he saw fresh tears in her eyes.

"I knew I shouldn't come up here. But he seemed like such a nice person." She blinked and then wiped wetness away. "I usually don't take to people quickly, but there was something so electric, so sudden, so fantastic about Cully. It made me chatter away like a fourteen-year-old. I...." She stopped and looked up.

"I've heard quite a bit about people wondering why Cully died. Were you his roommate?"

Mark nodded.

"What do you think? Was there some other reason that hasn't been brought out yet?"

Mark went through the gate and caught her hand. He walked across the campus with her and at last met her honest stare.

"Yes, Marsha, there is a lot more involved here than you know about, but in a week or two it will all be out in the open and you'll be reading about it. For right now it must stay this way: Cully got dizzy and fell off the balcony, no drugs were involved, no alcohol. He just fell."

She nodded seriously. "I don't know if that makes me more angry than I was. Before I could just blame some god or the fates or destiny. But now if there is some human being who is to blame...." She shook her head. "I just don't know."

"I'd appreciate it if this could be just between the two of us," Mark said. "We don't want to warn anyone."

"Oh, no. I'd never say a word." She smiled up at Mark, and it had almost been worth the risk. Almost. "If you learn anything else you can contact me at the pier. I'm usually there."

She got in her car and Mark watched her drive away.

Just six cars behind them, another interested viewer watched the girl's car leave and swung out to follow it. Mark had already turned and jogged across the campus toward the practice field. He didn't see the girl with large sunglasses and the long black hair. She smiled and congratulated herself on a masterful move as she followed the small blonde down the road.

Practice on the field was hectic. No one could catch the ball. They forgot signals. The coaches were not keeping their minds on the tasks at hand. At last Ben blew his whistle.

"Listen up. This has been a bad day for all of us. Cully's parents' name and address will be on the bulletin board. I expect each of you to send them a letter or a note. And do it today. We'll take the rest of the day off and get this out of our systems. Tomorrow we come back and start working twice as hard. Move it!"

When Mark got back to his room, he found a man leaning on the third-floor railing waiting for him.

"Wilson?"

"Yeah."

"Will Jones, San Diego Police." He showed

his detective's badge. "Understand you were the first one to get to Cully after he hit the ground."

"Right. I talked to the detectives last night."

"Could you tell me again? I've just been assigned."

"Special detail?"

The cop looked up quickly, then shrugged. "You Sharks are special to our town. We want to take care of you the best we can. What did Cully say to you when you bent down to him?"

"He didn't say anything, Jones. I was too late."

Jones nodded. "I know that's what you told them last night. Now, after the big press coverage has died down, is there a chance that you might remember something you overlooked? We have an eyewitness who says she thinks Cully moved and said something to you just before he died. Now, before you say anything, let me tell you that we know, and we're keeping it quiet, that Cully was working undercover for the commissioner of the National Football League." He said it softly so no one else could hear. "We know that something is going on in football that isn't good for the game, for the players, or for the fans. We'd like to help stop it if we can. We also know that there is no way you can make this team as a player, that you should have been cut after the first three days, and that Coach Sample told me that you are working as a special undercover investigator for him, personally. What I'm saying is that my job here is just as covert as yours. So let's work together if we can."

Mark rubbed his chin, then nodded. "Jones,

you look like you could use a workout. A little spare tire there. Could you stand a couple of laps around the track?"

Fifteen minutes later Mark had gone over the last moments of Cully's life and told Jones the last word Cully spoke.

"Brotherhood. Yes, we have a file on what the Commissioner knows. Which isn't one hell of a lot. Anything else you can tell me?"

"Nothing. But I want this killer. If we nail him we should be able to blast open the rest of it."

Jones stopped jogging and walked. Mark slowed with him.

"Oh, one more thing. We've had four men killed out in this area. Our organized crime people say all four of them were five-dollar gold piece-packing Mafia soldiers. You know anything about them?"

"Just what I read in the newspapers," Mark said.

Jones nodded, stopped and held out his hand. In it was a card. "Don't be a stranger. I'll help you any way I can. I hope that works both ways."

"You got it," Mark said. Jones nodded and walked toward his car.

7

Black Cat's Last Rite

Mark came up the far stairway to the third-floor dorm toward his room. On the second-floor landing he saw one of the veterans, a linebacker, he thought, not a starter. The kid looked surprised to see Mark and turned and went into the second-floor hall. On the top floor he found Dabrowski and Sparky Monroe. Both nodded and went down the steps, heading for their rooms below.

Mark thought nothing of it until he opened his door and saw blood on the floor as the panel swung open. He jumped inside, alert to the smallest sound, snapped on the light, and closed the door.

A black cat hung on the back of the door, spread-eagled and nailed in place, with it's belly ripped open and its guts hanging out. It wasn't quite dead and blood still dripped from its body.

The surprised faces of the three veteran players flashed through his mind. He usually came up the *other* stairs. They would have been waiting down there, out of sight, for his reaction. If they knew the cat was there, they must have put it there.

Mark left his room quietly. He remembered Dabrowski's room number, 104, on the first floor. He moved quietly and quickly and knocked gently on room 104. The door cracked open an inch and Mark's heavy shoe jolted it at the handle and rammed it inward. There was a shouted curse as a body tumbled over some furniture. The room was dark. Mark had stopped for one tool before he left his room and now he drew the .45 autoloader with his right hand and slashed upward with his left along the wall beside the door and flipped up the light switch. When the light came on he saw four men facing him. Their grins changed to stares of surprise, fear, and disbelief when they watched the black muzzle of the .45 semiautomatic pointing at them.

Mark closed the door with his toe and glared at the four veteran footballers.

"Gentlemen, this is where the shit stops! I don't give a good goddamn about that black cat you gutted on my door. But I'm mad as hell about a friend one of you killed by the name of Cully Ambrose." He saw startled glances from two of the men. Both were backup veterans who must have reported that day. The other two were Dabrowski and Sparky Monroe. Mark pointed his persuader at the two new men.

"You and you, when did you hit camp?"

"Today," the older one said, keeping his hands in sight, not moving quickly.

"Yeah, today," the younger one said. He started to get up.

"Stay!" Mark thundered and the sound of his voice jolted the player back on his chair. Mark watched them a minute. "Okay, then you couldn't be involved. This little charade doesn't have anything to do with either of you. My advice is to stand up slowly, move past me to the door, and go to your rooms and get to sleep. I don't want either of you to mention this happened to *anyone*, do you read me?"

"Yes, sir," the older man said.

"Yeah, sure, ain't my. . . ."

"Beat it," Mark said. They moved as he had told them, eased out the door and left. Mark locked it behind them.

"Monroe, did you push Cully off that balcony? You better think carefully before you answer me. You lie to me and I kill you right here. You tell me the truth and you have a possibility of a fair trial. Did you push Cully?"

"No, I swear," Sparky Monroe said, his face working, his hands trembling. "So help me, Wilson. I didn't know nothing about it till the damn ambulance came up. I live on the first floor."

"You ever come close to dying before, Sparky?"

"No, sir!"

"Stand up."

Sparky stood and Mark saw the warm dark stain spreading down the front of Monroe's khaki pants. "You do a hell of a lot better blindsiding rookies than you do killing. Get the hell out of here and stay in your room. In case anybody asks you, you were never here tonight, you didn't kill that cat, and you don't even know who Wilson is. Move it!"

Sparky did, carefully, slowly, going out backwards so he could watch the deadly weapon. When the door shut Mark locked it again.

Mark scowled at Dabrowski. "Now we come to the head honcho, the big sonofabitch who did both, killed the cat and shoved Cully off the balcony."

"No way, Wilson, you've got no proof," Dabrowski said.

"I've got all I need. I was *there!* you bastard. I *saw you* struggling with Cully and then push him over the side. There's a good light on that third landing. I *saw* you do it, you bastard, and now I'm going to kill you."

Dabrowski stood up slowly, his face worried. "No, no. Wait. It couldn't have been me, it was. . . ." He stopped. "It wasn't me, I swear. I'm just a messenger, no shit. Look, I know you're working on this Brotherhood thing. Christ, you've been asking questions of everybody. I'd have to be an idiot not to know that. But I didn't kill him. Sure I put the cat on your door, just a little prank. Happens every year to a joker who hasn't been cut and won't quit, who won't make the grade."

"Who do you report to? Who gives you your enforcement orders?" Mark asked.

"What the fuck you talking about?"

Dabrowski was sitting in a metal stacking chair all the rooms had, and Mark needed only two steps to be in front of him. Then his left hand shot out so fast Dabrowski saw it only as a blur as it slammed flat into Dabrowski's face, hard, crushing his nose and bringing a spurting flow of blood.

"Christ, what the hell?"

Dabrowski grabbed a shirt off his bed and held it over his nose. Mark moved again and the .45's muzzle pushed painfully upward, directly under Dabrowski's chin in the soft flesh between the jaw bones.

"You're about twenty seconds from dying unless you talk fast and straight. Did you kill Cully?"

"No."

"Do you know who did?"

"Not for sure."

"Fair enough, it keeps you living another few seconds. Who do you report to in the Brotherhood?"

"I don't. . . ."

Mark pushed the muzzle deeper into the tissue.

"Christ, easy. I can't tell you."

"Are you one of the two Brothers on the Sharks?"

"Hell, no."

Mark lowered the weapon. "Go to the sink and get your nosebleed stopped. Now."

He did and Mark was right behind him. Cold water did it in two minutes. Mark motioned him back to the bed. A phone sat on a stand.

"Call the man. Tell him you have a problem. Tell him he must meet me at the far end of the practice field at two A.M. That's a half hour from now. You don't have to tell me who it is, but be damn sure he comes. If he doesn't, you won't see another sunrise. Do you read me true, *bastard?*"

"Yeah. Right. I'm not stupid. I can tell you do what you say you do. Hey, I'll call him, he's got a phone."

Dabrowski looked at the door, then took a deep breath and sighed. He dialed and waited. It rang six, then seven times.

"He'll answer," Mark said.

On the ninth ring the other phone was picked up.

"This is Dabrowski. We've got trouble. Someone wants to meet you at the far end of the practice field in a half hour." He listened for a moment. "No, no way out of it. The man has a cannon pointing at me, you'd never get in the door alive. He means what he says. I've seen him operate." Dabrowski listened again. "Right, I'll try." He covered the mouthpiece.

"He says he can't make it in half an hour, how about an hour from now, two-thirty?"

Ambush, they needed time to set it up. Mark nodded. Dabrowski seemed relieved. "Okay, at two-thirty."

"Tell him to come alone and to shine a flashlight on his face under the goalposts on the far end. Any double cross and both of you wind up extremely wasted and dead."

Dabrowski relayed the message, then Mark nodded at him and slipped out the door and closed it, then ran silently down the hall and out. He expected men to pile out of one of the doors, but none came. They had a half hour to set up their ambush, and so did he. He ran upstairs and got Ava from his locked suitcase and ran back down the steps. He spent five minutes going around one of Coach Sample's night security guards, then drove his car to the far end of the practice field. He had both his .45 and Ava. The second weapon was a plastic-formed dart gun that could throw either sleep darts or lethal darts fifty feet with acceptable accuracy. The sleep darts contained a combination of strong tranquilizers and muscle-spasming agents, which threw the target into an uncontrollable shuddering that resembled a petit mal seizure and did it a second after the dart entered the skin and hit the blood supply system. The sleep tranquilizers took over ten seconds later and the trembling stopped. The target woke up in fifteen to twenty minutes depending on his body weight and defense systems.

Mark made a quick recon, determined three potential ambush sites close to the far goalposts, avoided them, and set up at the far edge of the field behind the linemen's sled and about forty feet from what he guessed would be the location of the first bushwhacker.

He settled down to wait. At ten minutes of two, the first man slid into the area, reconned it, and hid behind the single sled twenty feet from the goalposts.

Two more men came almost at once, and took up offensive positions at the other side of the goalposts, well hidden. One moved a pile of tackling dummies closer to the posts, then melted behind them.

At twenty-five minutes past two, Mark saw a golf cart come rolling silently down the track around the playing field. One man was on board. Mark took careful aim with Ava, using the red death darts, and put a silent shot into the closet ambusher's back. The darts were propelled with jets of CO_2 gas. Mark moved silently around the end of the field to the second hidden man and darted him in the arm. He cried out before he died, but the man on the golf cart didn't hear him. Mark was directly behind the third man and now crawled up to him quietly, plunged his stiletto into the man's stomach, turned it and ripped it out, killing him instantly. He searched the last man, and found a five-dollar gold piece and a folded-up sketch of someone. Mark put the sketch in his pocket and waited for the man on the golf cart.

Now, Mark watched the man at the goalposts and called for him to get off the golf cart and walk toward him. The man did.

"I have a .45 automatic trained on your big belly. You step the wrong way and you're dead. Now stop." Mark lifted from behind the tackling dummies and rushed up to the figure.

"Don't look for help from your three friends. They are all ready to feed the fishes in the best Mafia tradition."

The figure turned and ran. Even with the football player's speed, Mark caught him after ten strides, tackled him and then slashed the .45 across his head.

When they sat up Mark saw the messenger was Vic Dabrowski.

Mark pushed the .45 into his gut. "So you're one of the Shark Brothers?"

"No. They made me come. They sent some men, said all I had to do was walk up here, you would come out . . . and we wouldn't have to worry about you any more."

"They were wrong. You're just starting to worry about me. Come on, we've got some work to do."

Mark checked the other two corpses. All three were Mafia soldiers. He made Dabrowski load them on the golf cart. The big guard vomited the first time he picked up one of the dead bodies.

"You'll get used to it, dealing with the Mafia. They kill people all the time, including football players."

Mark had positioned his rental car at the end of the practice field. They timed their trip between the new security patrols, and Dabrowski loaded the stiffs into the back seat and the big trunk. Then Mark ordered him to drive.

"The idea is we get the bodies away from the playing field so the Sharks don't get any more bad publicity. That you don't need. I doubt if you'll be in shape for the first exhibition scrimmage against the Los Angeles Rams next Saturday at Irvine. You're looking a little green, Dabrowski."

They found a good spot along the glider-launching mesa next to the cliffs that dropped straight into the Pacific, and Mark told Dabrowski to dump the fish food into the sea. He did, groaning and throwing up again. When he had finished, Mark hit him with two karate chops alongside the neck that put him down on the closely clipped grass.

Dabrowski was a beaten man when he looked up.

"What the hell *else* do you want me to do?" he asked.

"You could start by telling the truth. Who did you call tonight?"

"No way, I'd be fish food by morning myself."

"You're about two pounds of trigger pressure away from the blue Pacific right where you sit. Or I could do it another way. I can testify that I saw you back in here tonight with a rented car and dump three dead men into the ocean. I can even find witnesses to back me up. You'd be pulled out of the practice field and slammed into a jail cell so fast your helmet wouldn't even fit. They might not convict you, but you would be so dirty after coming through a triple murder trial that no coach would touch you."

Mark toed the big guard, who shook his head. "No way I can tell you, or I'm a dead man for sure."

"Your choice, die now or die later. Okay, we do it by elimination. It isn't Fouts or Tilstrap, or you or Sparky. You want me to keep going?"

"Damnit to hell, I never volunteered for this

job. They just came to me one day and said I was it. No choice, do it or get busted up in the next game. I been busted up too damn much now."

"So talk. Who is one of the Brothers?"

"Christ, I'll be dead in two days. But that's better than right now. Tonight I called Frankie Vitale, a reserve back, specialist on kickoff and returns, an eight-year man, the little fireplug. Good old Frankie. How'n hell you think he got all the Mafia cooperation?"

"Is Vitale family or just well connected?"

"Hell, I don't know, ask him." Mark stared down at the hulk of a man lying on the grass. They were only two miles north of the campus and the dorm. "I should make you walk back to camp."

"You do and I won't even be able to get to practice tomorrow. We got a team to think about."

"You should have thought about that before you pushed Cully off the balcony."

"I told you, I didn't do that. One of the Brothers would have to handle that. I don't even know who the other one is. Only Vitale knows."

"So let's pay Mr. Vitale a visit."

"Not me, he'd kill me for sure. Hey, remember we got a championship to win this year."

"When I get through with the NFL there might not even *be* a season this year. All you big hitters will be on unemployment."

"Hey, man, don't even joke about something like that."

"On your feet, lard-ass, we're going to see Frankie Vitale."

Even in the thin moonlight, Mark could see Dabrowski pale.

8

A Don With Perfume

Carmine Lavangetti was furious, but he let only part of it show. He stared at her over the top of his glass, took a pull on the best bourbon he'd been able to find, and stood up. He was in his office in the penthouse at the Paradise Shores Hotel and Casino in Las Vegas. His baby sister, Angie, paced up and down in front of his desk on the deep pile carpet.

"You come in here and tell me you've lost seven soldiers and now you want some help? And you think, you just *think* that you have the Penetrator spotted. Christ, a fucking don in a skirt. I told Papa it would never work out. So he gives you half the family, and half the responsibility. You ain't even *married*, for Christ's sakes. How can you be Family or even Italian when you aren't married at twenty-six goddamn years old?"

Angie turned, her dark eyes snapping, as furious as her older brother.

"Carmine, I didn't come here for you to scream about the ERA and flex your goddamn gonads. I have the Penetrator tied down. I know the building, the *room* where he sleeps. But I need a little help. You packed me off to San Diego to run our nothing operation there and you sent me ten soldiers. You've got ten times that many. You know that sketch of the Penetrator they sent a few years back? I got one and duplicated it and spread them around. I've even seen the man *twice*, big brother, and it's him! It's the same man who charged through our house in Los Angeles all those years ago and murdered our friends.

"And I want him! I want to use a .45 and blast seven holes in his heart. Then I'll take his head and ship it to the *commissione* and collect my reward. I want him!"

"Seven men you lost. Seventy percent of your troops."

"Remember how many we lost in Los Angeles? Forty or fifty, maybe more. The very fact that I *did* lose seven men in two days should be proof enough that the Penetrator is in San Diego. He's at the Sharks football camp. I don't know what he's doing out there, but one of the players got killed."

"Yeah, I know."

She looked up. "You've got something going in my territory?"

"It's football, for Christ's sake. You wouldn't know a reserve punter from a first-string quarterback."

"Yeah, okay. But what about my help? I need

two crew wagons and a dozen men. I want them over there by tonight because we've got the capper planned. We'll take him out so fast he won't know what killed him."

"A lot of men have tried, and a lot of men have died."

"That's why I won't, I'm not a man."

He looked at the slinky low-cut dress that must have cost a grand. "I know, and in that dress you look like you're selling your ass. No good Italian girl would wear that."

"Brother, you let me worry about my own ass and who is selling what. Now do I get help or do I call Los Angeles?"

Carmine shot her an angry look and made a phone call. He gave curt orders and slammed down the phone. "They're moving. They report to you by phone when they get to La Jolla. They'll be staying at that Holiday Inn out there by the highway."

She grinned, ran up and kissed his cheek. "Thanks, Poopsie. That little pale-eyed wife of yours still putting out?"

Carmine pushed her away.

"You pop her twice a day and you'll have a kid before you know it. Just tell her to fuck Italian and she'll do good."

"Angie, you've got a filthy mouth."

"So look who my business associates are. Who's the crew chief?"

"Bobo."

"The same one?"

"There's only one Bobo."

"Yeah, he's your best man. I'll be careful of him."

Carmine stood and went over to her. "Hey, be careful. This Penetrator may look like an easy mark, but he's busted up half the Mafia families in the country. Just take care of yourself and don't get hurt. Send a crew in but you stay out of it."

"Yeah, sure, Carm."

"Look, I promised Papa nothing would happen to you. It was his idea to make you a half-don with the family here. You know what some of the soldiers call you when they're alone?"

She shook her pretty head.

"The Pussy-Capo."

She laughed. "I don't care what they call me, just so they know I'm boss."

"Some of them are saying you never even made your bones."

"That doesn't bother us, does it?" She put her hand around his neck and played with his hair. "Hey, you're still one of the sexiest Italian boys I know. You want to mess around?"

He jerked her hand away. "We're not fourteen any more, remember? Now come on, be serious. You go after that bastard Penetrator, you set it up right. No way out, no chance he can win. Don't take any risks."

She smiled. "Sure, big brother. Sure. I learned all I know from you, how can I lose."

She nodded, walked across the office twisting her tight little bottom as much as possible and waved at the door. "I'll let you know when I have the Penetrator's head in a plastic sack." She grinned and went out the door.

Carmine Lavangetti sighed, picked up the phone, and made another phone call. This one to his second-in-command. He told him to go to San Diego with Bobo.

"And don't let anything happen to my little sister."

"Right."

Carmine hung up and thought about the San Diego situation. He had done a friend a favor in the Shark camp and now it was getting hairy over there. Where did this Penetrator character come from? He remembered about him from before, but he hadn't done a lot to hurt any of the Families lately. Why now? And just how close was he getting to anything important on the Brotherhood? There was no way one hardcase was going to mess up the sweet thing he had going. No way! For a moment he wanted to fly to San Diego and take care of the matter person-ally. But he knew that wouldn't be smart, or practical. That's why a don had soldiers.

He worried about it for another half hour, then got back to his regular business of running a casino without the Nevada State Gaming Com-mission knowing anything about it.

Angie went to her suite on the top floor just under the penthouse. She had six rooms there permanently with a staff of two. She gave both of them the rest of the day off and called downstairs.

Ten minutes later the bell sounded and she went to the door. She wore only the briefest bikini panties and peered around the door, then nodded, and Tommy came in. He was twenty-one, with a lot of blond hair and a six-foot-two-inch body that was hard and firm as an oak tree.

"Angie! When did you get back?"

She closed the door, and he saw all of her and knelt and buried his face in her crotch. Then he picked her up and ran with her to the bedroom, where he tossed her on the big waterbed and dove on top of her.

"Oh, *God* but you make me feel good, Tommy! Us Italian women like to be roughed up a little, know what I mean?"

He turned her over and spanked her and she yowled with delight. It was going to be a delicious four hours until her plane left.

It was just after 4 A.M. when Mark picked the lock on Frankie Vitale's room and slipped inside. He too was waiting for a veteran roommate to report. Mark locked the door and looked around. He saw nothing out of the ordinary and snapped on the room's overhead light.

Vitale sat up in bed and shook his head as if he had just been body-blocked on a hard runback.

"What the hell?"

"Visitors, company time, Vitale. I was in the neighborhood and the family told me to drop by."

Vitale jerked his head up, instantly alert. His dark Italian features were pinched from trying to get his eyes closed down far enough so he could see something in the sudden blinding light.

"What? . . . Wilson. You damned rookie, how did you get in here?"

"Passkey, you never were much good on pass defense. Vitale, you know what this is all about."

"You're queer, a goddamned fag, and you want a blow job."

"Try again. Try murder. *You* pushed Cully Ambrose off the roof. I was *there*, you bastard. I saw you!"

"Old man, I knew you weren't a football player. So you're some kind of snoop. Who cares? Get the fuck out of my room so I can get some sleep. I don't know what you're talking about with Cully. The papers say he got dizzy and fell off. That's all I know about it."

"You're lying, Vitale, I saw you there. I'll testify to it."

Vitale leaned forward, his eyes angry now.

"Look, sombitch. I said I don't know anything about it. This is my ninth year in this fucking league. I just want to concentrate on getting in two more years. I got to make the goddamn team two more years, then I retire. All I got to do is make damn sure that the old knees hold together for a few more games. Now get the hell out of here or *I* call the cops."

Mark laughed. "Now that's good, a guinea soldier like you calling in the law. Hell, they'd take your five-dollar gold piece away from you."

Mark moved quickly to a dresser and picked up a gold coin. It was a five-dollar type, but when he turned it over it did not have the familiar Mafia embossment on it.

"I guess they don't really trust you yet," Mark said. "You're well connected, I can say that for you."

"So get the fuck out of my room."

"Or else what?"

"Wilson, I've heard you're handy with your hands and the karate shit. Don't try it on me. You're just a rookie shooting off his face, and I'm not the least bit worried about you."

"Those soldiers I've been bumping into, they yours, Vitale? You running San Diego now, or is it still mother-henned by Las Vegas?"

"I don't know what you're talking about."

"Figures. Vitale, one of these days I'm going to meet you when you can't hide behind your football uniform, and then I'm gonna knock over your fire-plug and see what kind of yellow gunk pours out of it. And then I'm gonna nail your ass for killing Cully. Yeah, yeah, you're right, Vitale. I could take you out anytime, right here, right now. But not this time. I want you in front of a judge and jury. I want to watch you sweat, and I want to see you look through the window at the press as you wait for that little cyanide pill to fall in the little green room. That will be one hell of a fine day, Vitale. Think about it." Mark picked up the telephone off the stand and tossed it at the running back.

"Call some of your Mafia friends. I can take on as many as you can send out here. Just remember, before this is done, I'm gonna burn down your ass one way or the other."

Mark flipped the surprised player a live .45 round and slipped out the door.

The Penetrator hurried out the first-floor hallway and across the lawn toward the far parking lot where he had left his car. There was no chance he would sleep in his room anymore. Things were getting too hot. He would drive away from campus and park and sleep. Better that than the alternative.

Back in the dormitory room, Frankie Vitale reached into a drawer on the small study desk and took out a folded sheet of paper. He opened it and stared at the drawing there. The forehead was too high and the eyes weren't right, but it damn well could be. The rest of the features, were about right. He looked at the bottom of the flyer and grinned. "This is the best composite sketch we and the various police agencies have of the man known as the Penetrator. The head money of one million remains. Anyone helping in the termination of this individual will be justly compensated. This is an open-ended arrangement." From the small hand-printed sign on the bottom he knew the flyer had orginated in Las Vegas. Frankie Vitale nodded. Damn right he would make a phone call. What the hell was his name? Yeah, Carmine Lavangetti. He would do nip ups. Call now or wait? Now, what the hell, for a tip like this, Lavangetti wouldn't mind at all.

The Penetrator found a quiet street in the edge of La Jolla and settled down in his locked car. He would get a few hours' sleep and report to practice almost on time. He wouldn't need any breakfast.

He took a few minutes to go over the whole web of events that was rapidly drawing tighter and tighter around the Brothers. Yes, it was narrowing. He could see some light through all the shadows.

It would only be a small strike against the criminal element, and again it would touch on the Mafia. There was no group the Penetrator disliked more. They were the ones who had thrust him into this business. He and Donna Morgan had been checking out his ancestory in the Los Angeles Hall of Records when they evidently opened up some files that were close to the Los Angeles Mafia organization. They were coming back from Big Bear when a team of hit men blasted their car off the road over a steep embankment. Mark was thrown from the car and lived. Donna was trapped in the flaming wreck and died in terrible pain.

Mark had swept out after the men who killed her. He took on the entire Los Angeles family and blasted them into dead men and burned buildings.

Now, he was as committed to upholding the American way of life as he had always been. But to give the American way a fair chance meant that the crime lords, the vicious racketeers, and the cancerous Mafia all had to be attacked and battered down and driven back and terminated whenever possible.

He would continue doing so until his last breath. And right now that meant rooting out this corrupt injure-and-kill mob that had almost taken over pro football. He would keep driving at them until he had blasted them into hell or into jail. Right then the Penetrator really didn't care where they ended up!

9

Day by Dangerous Day

Mark was called from the morning practice. They had just started to work on down and out passes when the team publicist came up to him on the field.

"We've got an emergency call for you from the San Diego police. Coach said you should take it. I have a number that you can call back. You're supposed to ask for Sergeant Hascall."

Mark shrugged. "Where's the nearest phone?" He took the slip of paper with the number on it and jogged over to a phone outside the gym, using the publicist's dime, and made the call.

"Good morning, San Diego Police."

"I have a call from a Sergeant Hascall. My name is Wilson."

"Yes, he said you'd be calling. Just a moment."

It was a woman's voice, low, soft. Not what he envisioned a lady cop to sound like.

"Yeah, Hascall here. This Wilson, Pat Wilson from the Sharks training camp?"

"Right."

"Good, been wanting to talk to you for a long damn time. You've got a problem, Wilson. You know a pretty little blonde by the name of Marsha, Marsha Day? She works out at the Scripps pier."

Mark's hand tightened on the phone until he thought he would crush it. The publicist looked over at him. Mark nodded at the PR man. "Just routine, some questions. I can take care of it." The PR man headed back to his temporary office.

"You hear me, Wilson? I said Marsha Day. Your little friend has got herself in a lot of trouble, know what I mean, Wilson? We figure that you'd want to help her. You understand?"

Mark's body trembled for a second with rage. This was not the police, it had all the classic trappings of a Mafia turkey shoot. He controlled his voice with a great deal of effort.

"Day, Marsha. Don't recall. I never forget a pretty face. She works where?"

"Don't bullshit me, Wilson. We know that you've met her, at least twice, and right now you're putting on an act that isn't working. I'll say this just once, so remember it. You have an hour to get out there and help her. She's in a grove of eucalyptus trees in that gully down from the UCSD library. There's no way to drive in there, you have to walk in on a lane that heads down from the far end of the parking lot. You be down that lane in an hour and you come alone. Maybe nothing will happen to her. It's up to you. But listen, you show up with some troops, or you bring in a chopper or the sheriff's birds, and all bets are off and it will be Marsha's last day. Get the picture? We've got something we want to discuss with you and we figured this would be the best way to do the job. It's now 10:32. You have until 11:32 if you want to see that pretty little bird still alive."

The line went dead. Mark left the phone booth on the run, slammed into the locker room, changed his clothes and ran for his rental car parked in the lot just below the gym. He knew the general area the caller talked about.

He swore at himself for ten minutes for being seen with Marsha Day. Once she had saved both Cully and himself on the pier, and then he walked across campus with her the following morning when Cully died. Now the Mafia goons had her, were using her as bait, and if the pattern held, she was already dead or wished that she were, Mark had no illusions that he was going in to save her. He was going in to *avenge* her.

From the aluminum suitcase in the trunk of the rental car he picked up the Ingram submachine gun and fixed a Sionics silencer on the muzzle. This Ingram was the 9-mm Parabellum model. He slung the weapon around his neck on a thin cord, put two more special thirty-round magazines in a hunting vest and picked up his .45 automatic and two extra magazines. He pushed two throwing knives in his half boots and shoved the hypodermic kit in the hunting vest and slammed the car out the driveway. Mark drove to a point just south of the UCSD library, parked and kept the Ingram under the hunting vest as he slid out of the car. He went through a protective shield of shrubbery, and came to the raw semidesert that San Diego becomes without life-giving water. He scanned the area ahead.

He was a little above the library still, and south. There was a finger ridge he could follow a short ways and then drop in a valley that was directly south of the small patch of eucalyptus trees the caller had mentioned. That would give him access with perhaps some surprise.

Satisfied with his scouting job, Mark took off at the trot that he used in the desert, where he could move at six miles an hour for ten hours. He saw no one when he slid into the sage and chaparral of the dry hillside. Then he was in the thicker growth of the gully and worked along the side of the slope to be free of the shrubbery. He checked his watch. Less than twenty minutes had passed since he had left the phone. If they were competent Mafia ambushers they would have their men in place before the call was made. He would wait and see.

Mark paused at the base of the eighty-foot upgrade and listened. He heard nothing but muted traffic from the highway a half mile away.

He moved up the slope easily and soundlessly, using his Indian training and heritage to glide up the hill with a minumum of effort while keeping his senses alert for the smallest sound. A rim of short, thick greasewood plants adorned the top of the small ridge, and Mark edged into them on his belly, looking down into the grove of eucalyptus trees. The Australian native trees had been brought to this country over a hundred and fifty years ago and flourished in the dry climate close to that of their native land. Now they grew everywhere without human help or extra water. The thicket below was made up of forty-year-old trees and generations of smaller ones. The big ones were fifty feet tall, waving in the gentle breeze and their bark peeling from the trunks in great scablike chunks.

He spotted the trail coming down the far side. There was a picnic table there, but no fire ring in the dry woodsy area. Mark picked out good ambush spots and began combing the areas carefully, looking for any sign of a human or of movement. A man moved a cramped arm to the left and Mark picked it up. The Mafia soldier was behind a fallen log fifteen feet from the trail. He pulled up his arm and checked a hand gun, then looked back up the trail. Mark was about fifty yards from him, all downhill, all through open country. No chance he could get close enough to be in range of the silenced Ingram.

With the first man spotted the other two were simple. He picked out spots where they would have a semi-cross fire without hitting their own men. A second ambusher was behind the big eucalyptus just in back of the picnic table, and the third man to the left crouched in an eroded wash.

He needed to be within twenty-five yards of the trio for accuracy with the Ingram. He looked at the line of trees downhill. It met with the valley he had been in two hundred yards below and worked back up to the grove with a thick growth of sage, greasewood, and other chaparral. Concealment, plenty to let him work up the hill within range. He picked out the big tree he would use, and made sure he could reach it without being seen by the trio. Then he moved at a trot back down the slope and along the side of the hill to the junction with the other ravine. He worked up through the brush quickly but silently. There were still ten minutes before the deadline. He moved with all his Indian skills, not crushing a branch, not letting a limb swing back. He ducked under and stepped over the growth, keeping low and not breaking a single dry twig on the ground. He paused and stood behind the first tree and checked the area. Yes, on course. Another twenty yards.

The Penetrator crawled the last twenty feet, the Ingram centered on his back as he used his toes and elbows to propel himself forward over the dry ground. He heard one of the men cough and a quick soft curse from the lead man. Then silence.

Mark stood behind his target eucalyptus tree and stared around it. Yes. He was within thirty feet of the center man, and about twenty yards from the other two. He wanted one of them alive. He picked the middle man and aimed the Ingram carefully, the heavy silencer on the nose acting as a balance.

The silencer chugged with a six-round burst and the man nearest the picnic table screamed and dropped to the ground with four of the 9-mm Parabellum slugs through his thighs. The other two bushwhackers looked back at their man briefly.

The Penetrator lifted the Ingram and sent a quick burst at the man behind the log. Four of the five deadly messengers burst into the gunman's chest, jolting him backward, rolling him into the dirt, the .45 dropping from his hand and his eyes staring upward at the bright sunshine without a blink or squint.

The third man jumped up and ran, only he ran toward Mark, since he had no idea from where the man was attacking them. The Penetrator waited and when the gunman was twenty feet away he edged around the tree, lifted the Ingram and sent ten rounds thunking into the Mafia gangster's head, chewing his face into unrecognizable pulp as the hot lead persuaders ground through his skull and brain, lodging there, churning the vital brain centers into mush and pitching the soldier backwards into the long sleep of death.

Mark looked back at the first victim who was screaming and trying to stem the flow of blood from his legs.

He still had the .45 in one hand.

"Throw down the piece," Marked barked at the hit man. He lifted it and sent a wild shot past Mark, who tightened his finger on the Ingram's trigger and sent six more rounds into the man's legs.

The scream came out a blubbering wail now, the gun fell from his hand, and Mark rushed forward and picked it up. Then he slapped the Mafia soldier twice on the face.

"Asshole, look at me!"

The man's pain-filled eyes came up, then the pain faded and anger prevailed.

"Where is she? Where is the small blonde girl?"

"No way, bastard!"

Mark slid the stiletto from his half boot scabbard and leveled it in front of the goon's eyes. The man was a murderer, he had to be to "make his bones" to join the Mafia. He deserved no sympathy, no mercy. Most men had a fascination and a terror of knives. They were virtually useless in torture for information, because of the fright factor. But for ultimate torture they were practical. By the same token, most men feared dismemberment as much as death itself.

"The girl, where is she?" He caught the man's hand, placed it fingers wide on a foot-long rock beside the man and positioned the knife over the first finger.

"I ask you once more, then I take your fingers off one at a time."

Fear surged in the face, then it was replaced by cunning.

"No way you'd do that!"

Mark lowered the knife against his first finger, then hit the back of the blade with the tough ball of his hand. The stilletto hammered downward through flesh and then bone and the lower two joints of the finger dropped to the ground.

The hoodlum screamed, his voice trailing off into blubbering gibberish. Sixty seconds later he shook his head, shivered, and with much effort stopped shaking.

"Where's the girl?" Mark asked again, his tone level, unemotional.

Stricken eyes darted to him, then down at the knife and his bloody hand.

"Oh, God that hurts. You bastard! Fucking bastard!" His eyes came up and Mark lowered the knife again.

"No! No! Not again. She's in a beach house in Del Mar. At twenty-seven-sixteen . . . no, no . . . at twenty-seven-oh-six Del Norte Street. White house, right on the beach. Damn, get me to a doctor!"

"Is the girl hurt?"

"She wasn't when I saw her an hour ago. Now get me out of here."

'I'll get you out of here and you won't hurt any more, fair enough?"

The Mafia killer looked up with a curious mixture of terror and understanding in his eyes as Mark lifted the silenced Ingram and sent a burst of six Parabellum 9-mm rounds thundering into the bushwhacker's brain.

Mark felt in the dead man's pocket and found the five-dollar gold piece, polished some blood off it, and put it in his own pocket. He turned and ran back down the gully under cover of the trees and brush and back the way he had come. If anyone were watching the trees with binoculars they wouldn't have seen a thing. And the silenced Ingram wouldn't have been heard more than a hundred feet away. The man's screams would be muffled. Mark had a chance, perhaps a half hour start on the backup men who would soon come down to see what happened to the hit team.

He hoped it was enough time to find the Del Mar address and Marsha Day.

10

Daylight, Daybreak,
Day's End?

The Penetrator drove by the Del Mar address, hung a right and then another and turned into the alley until he spotted the same white house, eased past it and parked one place away. Mark took Ava with him and the .45 in his shoulder leather under the hunting vest. He had replaced the spent magazine with a fresh one and let the Ingram dangle under his vest as he left the car. He carried Ava filled with six death darts and a fresh CO_2 cartridge. He walked in the rear gate, noticing that there was no window looking out on the back yard. To the near side was a back door, with fringes of sparse grass extending around both sides of the bungalow-type beach house. He tried the knob and found it unlocked. Carefully and quietly Mark turned the knob and edged the door open an inch so he could see inside. It was a kind of enclosed back porch.

Without a sound he slid inside and closed the door. Another entranceway lay directly ahead topped by a half-window. He ducked and moved up cautiously, then peered over the lower edge of the glass.

Kitchen. One man at a counter making a sandwich. Mark tested the knob and found it unlocked. He had to be sure: he couldn't kill an innocent man thinking he was a mafioso. Mark pointed Ava and her deadly poison-tipped dart at the sandwich maker, then pushed the door open farther and cleared his throat. The response was immediate and predictable. The man dropped the butter knife and jerked a .38 revolver from a shoulder holster Mark couldn't see.

The gun was in the soldier's hand when Mark fired Ava. The little dart hit his shoulder, the impact force injected the death juice into it, and the spasming agent took over well before the Mafia goon could pull the trigger. He went down with a low groan, crumpled on the floor without a sound, the gun jiggling in the hand that rested on his chest. Mark stepped into the room and took the gun from the man's fingers, and ten seconds later the soldier was dead.

Mark moved into the next room cautiously, but found no one there. A radio played somewhere upstairs. He went to the open stairway fitted along the inside wall of the living room and went up the old steps cautiously, using the inside edge of them so they wouldn't be so apt to squeak.

He heard voices above but didn't know if they were real or from the radio. At the top of the steps he found a short hall and two doors that opened off it. The radio music seemed to be coming from the closest one. The Penetrator passed it and listened at the second door. Nothing.

He decided to clear that room first. Slowly he turned the knob and eased the door inward. The room was starkly lit by the sun that streamed through the window.

The room was empty.

He moved to the second room and opened the door slowly just a crack. Inside he could see a bed but nothing else. He opened the door a little more. No one was in the room. A radio played on the dresser. On the bed lay what appeared to be a complete set of women's clothes, from bra and panties to shoes. He made sure no one was in the small closet, then went down the steps.

There was no one else in the house. He checked the other three rooms downstairs, then went back to the kitchen and stared at the corpse.

"Why didn't you tell me where they went?" he asked the body. Maybe he still could. Mark went to the living room and found the telephone. Beside it lay a pad of paper and a pencil. On the pad was a phone number. He stared at it a moment and checked it with the number the publicist had given him to call. The numbers were the same.

He called the San Diego police and asked for Sergeant Will Jones. He came on the wire almost at once.

"Jones, this is Pat Wilson. How about a trade?"

"Any day."

"You might send a unit into the draw below the UCSD library, to that little grove of trees. I heard some shooting down there. What I need is the address of a phone number. It may not mean anything and then it might, to me, not to you."

"This all connects up as the lawyers say?"

"Too damn well it connects up."

"Give me the number and hang on." Mark told him and Jones went off the wire, probably to another phone. He was back on in a minute.

"That's in a condominium in La Jolla." He gave Mark the street address. "It's listed under Nevada Enterprises Incorporated. The condo number is 1214. That's a high-class neighborhood."

"I'm a high-class guy."

"This shooting scrape, were you there?"

"Heard about it. A bad case of lead poisoning."

"All gents with five-dollar gold pieces in their pockets."

"The same fraternity."

"Not much loss. Anything else I can help with, Wilson?"

"When I need backup, you'll be the first to know."

Mark said goodbye and put down the phone. He went through the dead man's pockets and found a set of keys. He knew they would belong to the crew wagon in the drive. Outside Mark got in and started the big black Caddy.

Fifteen minutes later he was coasting to a stop outside the La Jolla Towers, a twelve-story condominium that somehow was built in spite of the California Coastal Commission. Mark parked the big rig in front of the main entrance and when a uniformed doorman came out he pressed a twenty-dollar bill in his hand.

"Won't be gone but a minute," he said. The

doorman nodded and Mark flipped the five-dollar gold piece in the air as he took the elevator up to the 12th floor.

There was only one listing opposite the 12th floor button, 1214. They had the whole damn floor.

Mark kept his hardware well under the hunting vest as he came off the elevator. There was a pair of guards sitting in easy chairs. Mark flipped the gold coin and they both relaxed.

"Hey, this the joint? I got pulled down here from L.A. for Christ's sake. What the fuck is going on?"

"Hell, nobody knows. We got a pussy don down here, you know that. You'll have to ask her yourself."

"I gotta check in? Fer Christ's sakes. I should be up north on something important."

One of the hoods chuckled. He pushed a button on his desk.

"Go on in and bitch to the lady."

"Which goddamned door?"

The door ahead of him swung open a foot and held. He went inside, closing it behind him and found himself in another hallway. A pair of doors opened in front of him and more were closed on each side. He drew Ava and held it behind him as he moved forward slowly, not sure what he would find.

A thin blond man sat at a desk. He looked up and frowned.

"We don't have any indication that Los Angeles was sending down anyone. Are you a messenger?"

"Look, I just follow orders. I get orders to come down here with a crew wagon, I come."

"Yes."

Mark flipped the gold coin and waited.

"Well, I guess we could put you up in one of the spare rooms and when Lavangetti comes back she'll talk to you. She probably knows what it's about."

"Hey, I got something going up in L.A. Know what I mean? How long's this gonna take?"

The blond young man stared at him coldly. "Now *you're* asking qestions."

"So I gotta know."

"Miss Lavangetti took a guest with her and a crew wagon and said something about going swimming at La Jolla Shores. She had a small blonde girl with her who must have been a family friend. They took two men with them."

"You know anything else about it?"

"No, I'm afraid not, now if you'll wait in the hall, I'll find a room for you."

"Hey, you made your bones?"

"Of course, stupid, now. . . ."

Mark shot him in the throat with an Ava death dart and he crumpled behind the desk.

In the hall outside Mark took out the two guards with the chugging of the Ingram. When he was sure both Mafia goons were dead, he took the elevator down to the first floor, pushed another twenty into the doorman's hand, and drove away from the classy condiminium, heading for La Jolla Shores.

They still had Marsha. Why would this Lavangetti woman take Marsha to the beach? A public beach? Were they going to make it appear as if she drowned? Three or four of them just beyond the breakers could easily come up missing one without the lifeguards noticing anything about it. Why the accident thing? The girl seemed to be in charge, a minor Mafia official who was a woman, a young woman of twenty-five or twenty-six. Then the seed of a rememberance grew in the back of his mind and he brought back the death of "Shoulders" Lavangetti, the boss of Las Vegas. At the time he remembered hearing that Lavangetti's son and daughter would be taking over the family. It must have happened. Another tie-in to Las Vegas.

He powered the big heavy car forward, back toward the public bathing beach just north of the La Jolla Beach and Tennis Club. The closer he got to the beach, the worse the idea of trying for a drowning seemed. It would be in front of hundreds, perhaps thousands, of people. And it would take Marsha's cooperation. Why else the clothes on the bed?

He ground down the hill to the beach and prowled around the parking lot, looking for another big crew wagon. He didn't see one. He toured around the lot once more, then he saw a big black Caddy shoot out from between two cars at the far end and come hurtling past him on the cross lane headed toward the La Jolla streets.

Mark spun the wheel and followed them. There was a flash of white teeth and long dark hair from the passenger's side of the other car and Mark was sure the woman recognized him. She was the same one he had seen at Black's Beach. The other driver headed for the freeway and once there slammed the Caddy to eighty miles an hour at once, passing everyone on the road. Mark stayed with them in the powerful big car. They missed the California Highway Patrol somehow, and careened onto an off ramp the other side of Del Mar somewhere and angled along a two-lane road toward the dry interior. Mark had the Ingram in his lap, ready to fire, but he assumed Marsha was in the car. He couldn't shoot except at the tires.

The driver slowed quickly and turned suddenly, and with a lot of driving know-how, spun the big car into a 180-degree slide so it was pointed back at Mark. The Penetrator twisted the wheel and hit the brakes, skidding so his big Cadillac stopped sideways in the road. He jumped out the door and watched the other rig come up. A handgun out the near side snapped seven shots at him as the other Caddy slanted through the gently sloping ditch at the side of the road and around the blockage and came back on the road. Mark waited for it to hit the blacktop, and then, from a prone position, hammered all thirty rounds out of the Ingram magazine, aiming the 9-mm slugs low for one of the rear tires. The left rear tire hissed and went flat and the car continued for twenty-five feet, then stopped. Someone was pushed out of the rear seat to the roadway, and the wounded car limped on down the road. Mark ran quickly ahead and found Marsha Day, crying softly, holding a scrape on her arm and thigh, but otherwise unhurt. She wore a soft yellow one-piece bathing suit, and looked up at him in surprise. Then she fell into his arms and all of the shock, anger, and fear drained out of her as her sobbing vented it to the world.

When she could get her breath and stop sobbing, she pushed back and wiped the wetness from her eyes.

"I'm sorry. I couldn't help that. And I don't even know your name. Were they really going to kill me?"

He picked her up and carried her back to the other Cadillac and helped her in the front seat.

"You were the bait in the trap. It sprung but it missed, so they were saving you for another trap. Then they would have killed both of us without a second thought. They're like that. Did you get the girl's first name?"

"Angie."

"Yes, Angelina Lavangetti. They're Mafia, did you know that?"

Her eyes widened. "My God! They *would* have killed us."

They drove back to the highway, got off at a service station access ramp and he made a telephone call.

Fifteen minutes later, in the parking lot of the Holiday Inn just outside of La Jolla, Mark met a San Diego unmarked police car and Detective Will Jones.

"Detective Jones, this is Marsha Day," Mark said.

He smiled. "Yes, the girl who saved Cully Ambrose the afternoon before he died. I talked to you on the phone."

"Oh, yes, I remember."

"Angie Lavangetti and some of her hoods kidnapped Marsha, held her against her will, repeatedly threatened to kill her, and assaulted her. After she files her charges, I want you to be sure she has a twenty-four hour police guard so they can't snatch her again."

Jones smiled. "That can be arranged. Are you telling me that the local Mafia people have some connection with Cully's murder?"

"Hey, you're the detective. I just want to be sure Angie can't get her hands on Marsha again."

"Done. Your tip on that grove of trees proved to be correct. You must have excellent ears to hear the shooting."

"Lucky." Mark wanted to move, to trade cars before anyone found the body on Del Norte Street back in Del Mar. Marsha stepped out of the car and came around and gave him a kiss on the cheek.

"Hey, when this is all over . . . maybe we could have a drink . . . or something."

"Maybe you could show me where the best fishing is off the kelp beds."

She smiled. "Name your species, and I can point out a dozen rocks and reefs and kelp paddies to provide the fish."

"It's a date."

He gunned away and saw in the rear-view mirror that she watched him, then got in the front seat of the patrol car.

Mark drove within a block of the Del Norte address and then slipped into the alley and walked past the white house. There was no special activity, no police cars, no stake-outs that he could spot. He eased into the rented car, turned the ignition and prayed the family hadn't wired a bomb to the starter. They hadn't. He pushed it into gear and drove sedately out of the alley and back to the parking lot a quarter of a mile away from the UCSD practice field.

That night he reported to the team's regular chalkboard sessions and no one commented on his absence during practice. Coach Ben Sample looked at him, paused for a fraction of a second, and then moved on. The coach wanted a report on what happened.

11

First Enemy Scrimmage

Coach Ben Sample was rounding into midseason form. He stared at the combined squads and his voice thundered.

"By God, we've been here a week now and even you rookies must have learned something. You have those playbooks memorized by tomorrow morning, because that's when we start hitting the competition. Tomorrow is our rookie squad scrimmage against the Los Angeles Elks up at their camp in Irvine. They've got some good people, but so have we. I'll need every rookie in camp, so work on any plays you're not sure of, on signals, patterns, and your assignment. We'll go up there. We leave here at 7:30 A.M. Now get out of here. Tomorrow we'll play a real game."

As Mark walked by him the coach crooked a finger at him, and the Penetrator waited in the hall until everyone else had left, then went to the Coach's office. He was alone.

"Come in and close the door. What the hell's been happening? Bodies have been dropping out of the goddamned sky around here. What are you, a one-man death squad?"

"I do what I can, Coach."

Sample sat down and tried to relax. "Anything new on the guys we're hunting?"

"A little. I'm working up their chain of command. There are two Brothers on each team, and each one of them might have one or two helpers. I think one of the two Brothers pushed Cully off that balcony. But I can't prove anything yet."

"Keep digging. And I want you to stay with the squad. I'm low on rookie tight ends, so I might need you tomorrow."

"Coach, you're kidding. I missed practice yesterday."

"Kid, I'd rather let you miss a signal than have to put in one of my veterans and get him chopped up in a scrimmage that means nothing. Hell, you wanted to play. You're not afraid of a little contact. Most of these guys are college kids."

"You know how hard these young college kids hit." Mark grinned. "Okay, Coach, I'll watch for any dirty tactics. Isn't this the setup where each team has the ball for thirty plays?"

"Right. As long as a team makes first downs they get to keep the ball, but we even it out at thirty offensive plays each. Now get out of here and get some sleep."

Mark did, in the nearby Holiday Inn. He had a shaver in his emergency suitcase in the car's trunk. He wasn't about to sleep in his room at the dorm, and he wanted a better night's rest than he could get in the car.

The following morning he reported to the breakfast line at the cafeteria and found the team in good spirits. After a week of nothing but theory and teaching and training, they would get a chance to show off some of their skills.

The team bus ride reminded him of the crosstown games at UCLA and then they were on the field, and some of the old thrill came back, in full pads and helmet and even a jersey with his name on the back. That was for the benefit of the coaches. He watched the kickoff and then settled back on the bench, checking the play, looking for anything that was out-and-out vicious, but saw nothing as the Elks rookies drove down to midfield and then kicked the ball. On the tenth play of the Sharks' first drive, the rookie tight end, Beloit, caught one over the middle and had his bell rung by the inside linebacker and the cornerback both at once.

"Wilson!" the offensive coach shouted and Mark trotted onto the field, snapping his chin strap. In the huddle the rookie quarterback, Hammershaw, grinned at Mark. He was a tall black kid from Alabama, sure to be a star in a few years.

"Twenty-seven slant out, on two. Wilson, that's you. Fifteen yards downfield on the side stripe. That's where the ball's going to be, you be there to get it."

Mark nodded. They all clapped and ran out of the huddle.

Mark bounced off his blocker, ran straight

downfield ten yards, dipped inside, then cut hard to the outside and looked over his shoulder two yards from the out-of-bounds marker. The ball was there, he gathered it in, cut to his left along the stripe, and made another ten before the safety pushed him out of bounds. It was a twenty-four-yard gain.

"Not a bad throw, Hammershaw," Mark said back in the huddle.

The quarterback was watching the sidelines where two men were sending in signals for the next play.

It was a fullback sweep left and Mark lined up on that side and cut the big defensive end's legs out from under him, rolling over on him when he tried to get up and follow the play.

Before the next play the other tight end came jogging across the field and Mark ran for the sidelines.

Coach Ben Sample whacked him on the rump and held his shoulder pad as he went by.

"Wilson, you trying to make my coaching staff look bad? They all said you should be cut tomorrow morning."

"I got lucky, I'll probably drop the next one."

"Wilson, in this league, twenty-four yards ain't lucky," the offensive coach said as he walked up. "It's a damn miracle."

The game battered up and down the field as the rookies, free agents, walk-ons, and enough veterans to fill in the holes extended themselves to show the coaches they could really *play* the game, not just look good in practice.

At the half the Elks rookies had the edge

seven to thirteen. The locker-room time between halves was cut to fifteen minutes and the teams stayed on the field, grouped around various coaches, getting chewed out and instructed.

"What the hell you mean you *forgot* the signal, Culver? That five yards offsides cost us a touchdown. Next time you watch the damn ball if you miss the signal. Go a fraction late, not early. On the way home you're gonna tell me the snap count on every play in the damn book."

Mark checked with the other rookie tight end, and found him anxious to be in the game for the second half, it was his turn. The Sharks already had two outstanding tight end veterans, one all-pro, and another four-year man. They might carry one more if he could double somewhere. Most of the rookies playing today would be cut, but some might find a spot in the USA League next spring. Somebody said there were over ten thousand football players graduated from college every year. The NFL signed maybe a hundred and fifty of them. The odds were horrendous.

In the second half Mark saw one vicious, slashing block away from play and the man was called for unnecessary roughness. The Elk coach sent the player to the showers at once. Mark saw nothing else out of line all afternoon.

Late in the fourth period the Sharks were ahead twenty-one to twenty.

"Wilson, get your ass up here," the offensive coach yelled.

Mark grabbed his helmet and jogged up to the coach.

"Let's see if you really can play this game.

You're getting the ball four times in a row. This is your big chance."

"My big chance to get killed," Mark muttered as he ran across the field to the huddle. As the game progressed and tightened, both coaches threw in some of their experienced defensive players. Now the Elks had about half of their veteran defensive platoon on the field.

Hammershaw wasn't in, it was some other rookie with less hype but with a skinny rubber band for an arm. The book on him was that he threw hard, but he could put the ball right on your letters.

Mark heard the call for the first play. It was him, a slant from left to right over the center. It was designed to pick up nine or ten yards. They needed eight on this second down. Mark hit his assigned incoming man, bounced to the inside and roared over the center, looking back a second before he thought he needed to. The ball hit him in the chest and almost bounced away, but he grabbed it, pulled it in and covered it with both hands as the inside linebacker met him head on and he stopped in mid-stride and bounced another yard upfield on the way into the grass.

But he held on to the ball.

It was first down.

The quarterback looked at him in surprise as the next call came. It was a deep delayed post pattern, with Mark blocking his man, then leaving late and getting in the seam behind the linebacker and the safety about twenty yards downfield. Mark stayed with his man, the quarterback scrambled to the right, then Mark flew downfield, put two moves on the linebacker and was past him, then looking back. The quarterback was in trouble, but got the ball away, a bullet that flew almost forty yards downfield. Mark saw the left cornerback coming, knew he was going for the interception. Mark stopped and moved back two steps and went high in the air, cutting the cornerback out of the play, coming down with the ball and doing a fake left and right and then going around the all-pro cornerback like he was a rookie, blasting the last forty yards down the middle of the field for the score.

Mark slammed the ball into the ground, then grabbed it and ran off the field as he saw no handkerchiefs on the turf and the official in the end zone raising his hands, signaling a touchdown.

Back on the sidelines the rookies and veterans alike were giving him a high five and slapping him on the back. The offensive coach did the same, then scowled.

"How the hell did you get by Baker? He's an all-pro corner back. Nobody goes past him and makes him look foolish that way."

Mark laughed, feeling wonderful. "He just had an off day, coach. He didn't take me seriously."

"Hell, he better and so had a lot of others. So far you're my number three tight end."

Immediately Mark could feel the shift in attitude among the players. The veterans nodded at him now. One of the veteran tight ends gave him an upright handshake and a comment about his nice move after catching the ball. For just a moment Mark gloried in it. Maybe he *could* make it for a season as a pro footballer!

Then he came back down to earth, remembered the dozen Mafia hit men who must be lurking out there somewhere, just waiting for him to show his face again. No, there was no chance he could ever be in a high-visibility business like pro football. And he knew day in and day out he couldn't make the grade against all this talent, body size, and determination. A twenty-one-year-old talented kid six-four would come along and nudge him to one side. He'd had his moments of glory on the 100-yard-long field. Now he had more important work to do.

The Penetrator grinned on the bus on the way back to San Diego. At least he had turned the tables and upset the averages with Marsha Day. He had got to one of the victims before she became turkey meat. That didn't happen often. Perhaps it was just an incompetent bunch of Mafia goons here in San Diego.

The football fixers came first. Then, if he had any time and energy left, he would see how he could punch some more holes in the local and the Las Vegas Mafia types.

Mark kept going over his progress on the Brotherhood. There had been no obvious work by the group today that he could detect. The one vicious, dirty hit today had been by a player who had a reputation in camp for being a little over the edge, one with personal problems who seemed to take them out on other players.

Beyond that, the day had been worthless in terms of the Brotherhood. Mark evaluated his position carefully on the ride. He had routed out one man he figured was in the Brotherhood with the Sharks, but so far he hadn't penetrated further. Where did it extend upward from there?

Frankie Vitale was a hard nut to crack. He would play it all close to his chest now, not take any chances, and be in on the payoff. What Mark needed was that vital link between Vitale and the big shots who ran the whole operation. It would be hard to beat it out of Vitale. Mark had a strong suspicion that if he researched it he could trace Vitale back to one of the old-line Mafia families. They were letting him have his kicks playing pro ball until he was through, then he would settle back, retire from football and front one of the family's big legitimate firms that hid their dirty money. Mark didn't have time to fool around with Vitale. A week from today was the first exhibition game, and he wanted everything wrapped up before then. He needed to give Vitale some rope, blast him into action somehow. Maybe a phone call would help. For a minute he thought of moving back into his room. No, with Vitale's connections the man might have a fragger he could toss into the door late one night. Mark had to tempt Vitale, then pull back and vanish, then tempt him again. Yeah, a phone call might do it. The good old phone call bit.

12

Off With His Head!

Mark left the bus and walked with the others back to the dorm, then slid past it out the far door and found a phone booth. He left the door open so it would be dark and he could see all the way around. He called the number he had memorized from Frankie Vitale's dorm phone the night before.

It rang four times before someone picked it up.

"Yeah?"

"This Vitale?"

"No, you want him?"

"Damn right."

A minute later Vitale came on the line.

"Yeah, man, Vitale here. Who's this?"

"What the hell you mean, who's this? We give you a little job to do over there and you fuck up. We got cops crawling all over us here. You get your act together, asshole, or we make you quit playing games and get to work. You hear me, little brother? Now, I don't want no more of your bullshit. You do it like it's supposed to be done or I'm pulling your goddamned plug! Get with it. Now I got an important call coming through. You get with the program!"

Mark hung up at once before Vitale could get in a word. He grinned. It might help. He would see what went down. In the meantime he could use some sleep. He'd find a new motel tonight. There were plenty around, and Vitale and his boys would never find him. The Penetrator left the phone booth and jogged back toward the gym and the far end of the big parking lot.

He would have beaten them there if he'd gone straight to the motel. Instead he detoured around one of the other classroom buildings just to look at it. They didn't make classrooms or college buildings like this when he was in school. It was beautiful, with clean flowing lines, an interesting mix of bricks and glass that was still functional. He had been equally impressed with the cliff hanging of the library where it surged outward in geometric shapes and angles that made it look like a building from some distant, fuzzy future.

When he came to his car he took a precautionary look around, saw no one, and put his key in the lock.

"Hey, asshole!" someone called behind him.

It was the kind of greeting that calls for some kind of response, and Mark turned around, alert, curious. Someone stood up from the shadow of a car behind Mark and pointed something at him that looked like a gun. There was no time to get a weapon from the aluminum suitcase; no time to duck, dodge, or defend himself.

The device fired, and he knew it wasn't a regular gun. Something struck him in the chest, penetrating his thin shirt.

Strong, needlelike, barbed probes drilled through his shirt into his skin, lodging a quarter of an inch into his flesh, two of them, and at once he felt the electric jolt. He rumbled and shook and trembled with continual electric shocks and fell to the ground.

He was conscious, knew what the three men were saying, and the pain was intense though it was not the brutal high wattage he associated with a 120-volt household wiring shock.

His whole body jolted and shook and rumbled with pain as the man ran up and then Mark could see the small wires that were still attached to the gunlike device with the heavy battery pack over a shoulder.

Tasar! The electrical stun gun some police departments were using now on violent persons. The pain increased and the men turned him over and handcuffed his hands behind his back. Mark was alert enough to expand his wrists with all of his muscles still in control. He felt them tie his feet.

"Hell, easy!" a thin high voice said. "I told you it would work, Vitale, I told you!"

"Shit, this was easy. A .45 would have been just as good, but a lot more noisy. Get him into the pickup and let's get out of here."

Mark felt himself lifted and dropped into a pickup box, then two men got in with him and the rig started and drove slowly out of the lot and up the highway. He couldn't see where they were going. As soon as he was in the pickup they had unhooked the power supply to the two electrodes that had shot him, and the electric shock and the debilatating pain stopped.

It was like being reborn. He had the use of his muscles again. He could flex his arms, move his legs.

He could smell the salt air. They must be near the coast. When they pulled him out of the pickup he saw Vitale and Sparky Monroe. He didn't know the other two. They were in a hilly residential section, maybe Del Mar or Solano Beach.

Sparky shied away when Mark looked at him.

Vitale shrugged, grabbed Mark's shoulder and propelled him into a small stucco house. "It don't matter what he sees now. It won't matter at all."

Inside the house they put him on a couch and watched him.

Vitale sat by a phone and scowled, then dialed a remembered number and Mark knew it was long distance by the number of digits he pressed.

"This is Vitale in San Diego. I need to talk with the man." There was a pause. "Well, *find* him and tell him I have to talk. No, it can't wait."

Vitale drummed his fingers on the coffee table as he waited.

"Christ, you'd think Bartholemue was a god-damned duke or something. I'd like to have him in the family for just a year."

He kicked his feet down from the low table and moved the hand set.

"Bart, yes, it is me. Wanted to report that the little problem we'd had with our public relations down here is all cleared up. I have the man who was doing the damage, and he won't bother us any more. Right, he's going fishing for a spell, which means we can get back to work on the important stuff. You have anything for us in the first game?" He listened. "No, not the exhibitions, the first league game, the opener."

He listened, laughed softly. "Yeah, right, we'll take care of it."

Vitale put down the phone. He took out one of the fliers with the sketch of Mark that had been circulated and showed it to the Penetrator.

"They made a very good likeness of you, Penetrator. The only problem is you're going to lose your head over it." He laughed. "Two million, cash. Christ, I can put it in a bank and live off the income for the rest of my life. Two million at even twelve percent would be about two hundred and fifty thousand a year. I could live on that. Travel around. Damn! And it would set me up for life in the Family. Christ, I could do just about anything I wanted to!"

The three other men were grinning.

They got back in the pickup and drove again. When they stopped this time, Mark saw they were at Torrey Pines State Beach just south of Del Mar. It's a three-and-a-half-mile-long sandy beach park mostly below the 200-foot-high eroding cliffs along the beach. The beach is accessible only by walking from one end or coming down the treacherous cliffs on unofficial trails that lead to Black's Beach on the north end beyond the state-controlled area, where the city handles the security on the mile-long stretch of Black's Beach.

After dark almost no one was on either beach. Driving on the beach was not allowed, but they tried, found the stretch of soft sand too soft, and backed out quickly before they became stuck.

"So we walk," Vitale said. "Our big pass-catching hero here won't mind one last mile walk."

Mark had been busy on the ride. He knew with certainty that Vitale was intending to kill him. Now was the time. He applied all of his *Sho-tu-ca* skills and overrode pain and worked on his handcuffed wrists. When he had expanded his wrists as the cuffs were going on, it meant they hadn't clicked down as tightly to the bone as they should have. Now by relaxing those formerly expanded muscles and scraping the steel against bone, he could work his hand part way out of the left cuff. He worked every minute of the ride and by the time they stopped on the beach he had his bleeding left hand almost out. He gave one more final jolt and forced his thumb and his thumb knuckle out of joint and through the metal, scraping off a quarter of an inch of flesh and bruising the thumb bone. He held the loose cuff in his left hand as they pulled him out of the pickup and in the darkness no one could see his left hand undone. They had to untie his legs so he could walk.

As far as he could see, only one of them carried a gun, Vitale, and he had it in his pocket now. The two goons probably had pieces but he hadn't seen them yet.

"How fucking far we got to go down here?" one of the big men asked.

"As fucking far as I say," Vitale shot back. "Watch your mouth, Bruno, or you'll be back in Detroit knocking heads and freezing your ass off."

They walked another quarter of a mile. There was no cover, just the empty, moonlit beach, the crashing waves, and the nearly vertical eroding cliffs on the land side. Now that the tide was out, there were two to three hundred feet of sand between waves and cliff. Not good odds. But time was running out.

Mark stopped walking.

"Vitale, no need to put me to sleep with the fishes. How about a deal?"

Vitale stopped and turned, then walked back two steps and lifted his hand as if he was about to say something. Mark exploded with a slashing, vicious kick to Vitale's crotch. His foot found its mark and Vitale screamed and grabbed for his revolver. Mark swung his right hand like a scythe, the fully closed cuff dangling on the short chain slammed into the first goon's head, and Mark felt the blood and tissue splatter on him as the man crumpled to the sand. Vitale had given up going for the gun, he was lying on the edge of the wet sand, his legs pulled up to his chest, screaming. Two down, two to go. Mark whirled and saw Sparky diving for him in an all-pro tackle. Mark lifted his half boot and caught the flying Sparky flush on the forehead with the heel as the tackle arrived. The force of the weight drove Mark backward, dumping him into the sand. He rolled and came up at once, but Sparky lay where he had fallen. The second hard man, Bruno, still fumbled for a weapon in his belt. It had snagged on a sweater he was wearing.

Mark ran at him and jumped, thrusting out both feet in a killing drop kick that landed just over the Mafia soldier's heart. The big man went down in a heap, his hand pulling the revolver free, but it dropped to the sand. Mark fell to the sand at the end of the drop kick, lunged for the gun and scooped it up, then ran over to Vitale. The Penetrator kicked the handgun away from the Family man's clutching fingers and then threw it far out into the breakers. Vitale still couldn't walk. Mark quickly checked the other three. The soldier with the head wound was dead. Mark took a .45 from him and checked the magazine. Full. He threw the revolver he had into the surf.

Sparky Monroe was sitting up, groggy. He had no weapon.

"Monroe, with that hard head of yours a tap like that won't hurt you. Stand up and start walking. You'll come to the Scripps pier in about three miles, then take a left and you can get back to the campus. Move it!"

Sparky stood, shakily, stumbled once, looked back and then walked forward, south along the beach. He swore softly.

"Asshole, you're lucky you're alive!" Mark flung at him. "If I thought you were more than a dupe, you'd be dead."

The second soldier had expired as well. The double kick blow to the heart had been enough to stop his pump. Mark checked him and fished in both front pockets, finding the five-dollar gold piece in the left one. He left it there.

Mark had taken the pickup keys from the right pocket and he kept them, then moved back to Vitale.

The Penetrator pushed the .45 into Vitale's stomach where he sat on the dry sand.

"Vitale, I'd say you better cash in any idea of making it to ten years in the league before your retirement."

"You bastard!" Vitale spat out.

"Sticks and stones and .45 slugs, Vitale. Remember that old one? Let's talk about Bartholemue."

"Go fuck yourself."

"There's a Bartholemue called Bart who is a defensive line coach for the Elks. Same man?"

Vitale looked away. Mark was standing, looking down at the wide receiver. The Penetrator kicked gently at his crotch and Vitale exploded in screaming pain.

Mark sat in the sand and waited. When the screams subsided, and Vitale's hatred-filled eyes focused on him again, Mark went on.

"We were talking about Bart Bartholemue. Elks?"

"You'll have to kill me, you bastard. I won't tell you a fucking thing."

"You will, Vitale, you will. And in the morning you'll be found here, dazed, half-unconscious, handcuffed to two dead men. It will make an interesting story for the newspapers. Not light reading, and *not* for the sports pages. But what the hell, Coach Sample has two high draft wide receivers. He's fat in that department and you've slowed down two steps. That's the death knell for a flanker."

Mark sat there a minute. "For a Family member you're as soft as an old woman, Vitale. The Lavangettis must be laughing themselves sick right now. Angie is counting on that head money. And by now big brother Carmine will be in it up to his elbows. And you goofed. Hell, you probably never even made your bones."

"Fuck I didn't!"

"That's what I hoped you were going to say, Vitale. It makes the rest of this just that much more pleasant."

Mark slammed the side of the .45 against Vitale's head, plunging him into unconsciousness. The Penetrator found the handcuff key in Vitale's pocket, transferred one of the goons' five-dollar gold pieces to Vitale's pocket, then dragged the three men together and forced one handcuff to hold both Vitale's slender wrist and the larger one of the first goon. It barely made it. Mark put the other soldier on the pile and made sure they were far enough up on the dry sand to miss the high tide. Then he jogged down the beach to the pickup at the end of the parking lot. He wanted to put a torch in the gas tank and let it blow, but then he would have to jog back to his car, and right now after the game and the exertion here it seemed too far. He also needed the first-aid kit that he had in his emergency suitcase. Mark got in the pickup, and drove it back what used to be the old Highway 101, the main link to San Diego and Del Mar before freeway 5 went in. He drove up what was now called North Torrey Pines Road to the university. He left the pickup in a lot a quarter of a mile from his own car and ran to it cautiously. They had found it before. There seemed to be no guard. He checked under the hood, but saw no obvious dynamite bomb and got in and started it. Mark drove to a motel in Pacific Beach, registered, then bandaged his left hand. Now he couldn't park on campus anymore. They knew his car. He wondered about calling Sergeant Jones with a tip about the two bodies, but decided he'd let the regular beachcombers find the trio, probably soon after daylight.

Mark settled down to evaluate the situation. He had one Shark Brother nailed, what about the other one? Or should he visit Bartholemue at the Elks' Camp in Irvine? He'd sleep on it.

13

One Break at a Time

It was 10 P.M. when Mark phoned the number Detective Jones had given him. The phone was answered at once.

"Pat Wilson calling Jones. How is Marsha Day?"

"Fine. We have a policewoman with her. She insisted on going to work and living at home. A feisty little person. But she's safe. I have her home phone if you want to check." He gave it to Mark. "Hey, Wilson, I'm still damn curious how you always seem to know where the next bodies are going to turn up."

"Excellent hearing and a nose for news. I used to work a newspaper crime beat."

"Really?"

"No, I just made that up. I want to call Marsha. Thanks." Mark hung up without saying goodbye, and punched up the number he had just received.

"Yes, hello."

"Hello. You must be the cop Jones told me about. Is Marsha there?"

"Who is calling, please?"

"Wilson, Pat Wilson."

"Yes, you scored a touchdown today. Nice play. I don't see how you got around Baker, though. He's all-pro."

"Yes, Miss, he certainly is."

"Oh, here, Marsha."

The voice that came on the line was tentative, a little surprised.

"Hello, Pat?"

"Yes, Marsha. Just checking to be sure the flatfeet are taking good care of you."

"Oh, yes, they are marvelous. I've never felt so safe since my mother walked me to school that very first day."

"Good. I wanted to check."

"Hey, I don't have a phone number for you."

"Anything important, have your lady cop tell Dectective Jones. I bother him every once in a while."

"Good. When . . . when this is all over, Pat. . . ." She paused and he heard her take a deep breath. "When this is all over I want to see you. I haven't even said a proper thank-you for saving my life." She stopped. "I *really* want to, Pat."

"Fine. After this is settled. I thought we had a date to go fishing."

"Yes, that too, of course."

"Good. You stay healthy, and don't take rides in strangers' cars. I'm counting on that fishing trip."

She laughed softly and he enjoyed the sound. "Mr. Wilson, you can absolutely *count* on that, by pole and line, or mask and fins or scuba."

"I better go. Take care of that lady cop."

They hung up and Mark sat for a moment remembering the small soft face, the billowing blonde hair and the neatly trim body. He was looking forward to that fishing trip, but first there were a few problems.

Bait. Bait in the trap. Only this time he would be the bait in his own trap. It might be the quickest way to sniff out the other member of the Brotherhood, and he'd have to do it tonight. He put his gear together, went out and got in his rented car, drove back to the closest parking lot to the dorm, and took his bags upstairs. He made it a point to talk to several of the veterans on his way into the dorm and up the steps. One even commented on his catch. On the third floor he found three open doors and couldn't get past the other rookies without talking for a while. The drift seemed to be that he had the inside line on winning the third tight end spot on the squad. He got to his room, found the key still worked and went inside. Nothing had changed. The detectives had left everything just as it had been on his side of the room. Cully's gear was all gone.

He left his door open for a while too, then he heard people saying good night and the noise level dropped as tired players dove into bed. About eleven he closed his door, turned on a small radio, and then built a reasonable-looking dummy from pillows and a blanket roll in his bed. On the pillow he put a Shark billed cap to cover the spot where the rest of his head should be.

He looked through his aluminum suitcase for several minutes before he picked out exactly what he wanted.

He found it on the bottom of the case, a kind of supermace mixed with ether. The mace put you down and a second squirt of the pressure can would leave the victim unconscious for ten minutes. The advantage it had over Ava in close quarters was that he could use it on three or four people at once. Mark slid Ava into his belt holster and his .45 under his shirt on the right in his clip-on leather.

Mark unscrewed the bulb from the overhead light so the wall switch wouldn't work, then turned on a small night light that left the room nearly dark. He locked his door and then turned off the night light as well, and leaned against the wall on the hinge side of the door.

Soon he sat in a straight chair, and Mark drifted into patrol sleep, that combat state when you're almost asleep and your body is resting, but your mind is in slow motion. The slightest little sound or movement snaps you alert at once, ready for action both mentally and physically. He had used it many times in combat in Vietnam and since then in life-and-death situations. Mark guessed that it would be sometime after midnight before any strike would come. He also guessed that the absence of one Brother would alert the other one, who undoubtedly had been in communication with his shadow agent.

Mark jolted up when a car backfired in the lot less than a hundred feet away. Later two men came in from a party with an assistant coach herding them.

At 2:30 something touched his outer door and Mark was alert, the heavy-duty spray can up and ready. The person used up almost a minute picking the simple lock, then the door opened a few inches and the wall light clicked. When nothing happened the door came open farther and a figure slid through, then closed the door. A small flashlight snapped on, aimed at the bed, and in the shadows Mark's *Sho-tu-ca* night sight showed him the figure of a large, heavy man with a mask on. His light centered on the bed and a moment later his other hand came up with a silenced weapon. It coughed quietly four times and the slugs ripped into the dummy on the bed. Mark couldn't risk the spray. He shot the man with an Ava sleep dart, saw the big form sag, then growl in disbelief as the spasming agent hit his nervous system and his arms and legs went out of control and he fell heavily to the floor. Mark eased around him and opened the door. No one was in the dimly lighted hallway. He was a solo operator. Mark closed the door, locked it, and put a chair under the handle.

By the time Mark screwed in the top light bulb and took the mask off the big man, he had lapsed into a tranquilized state. Mark stared down at the black face. He was Ira Ronkowski, starting offensive guard, a talented veteran in his fourth or fifth year. He would be missed.

As Mark waited for the player to come out of his short sleep, the Penetrator dropped the magazine from the .45 Ira had used, ejected the round from the chamber, and looked at the piece. It was an Army-type .45 with an expensive silencer with which he wasn't familiar. It had a round snout an inch in diameter and almost eight inches long. Mark took two filled .45 magazines from his weapons case, jammed one of them into the silenced heavy handgun and pushed it inside his belt. Mark wondered if he would need any other tools, decided he wouldn't, then changed his mind and took two packs of cocaine and heroin from his aluminum case and pushed them into his pocket in case he needed to plant some on Ira.

Twenty minutes later, Mark and Ira were doing wind sprints on the practice field. There had been a few anxious moments when Ira woke up and found himself gagged, and both his hands and his feet fastened with plastic riot cuffs. But Mark convinced him that if he didn't want to die right there, he would have to come to the practice field where they could settle the problem man-to-man to .45.

They ran three fifty-yard sprints down the field and back and halfway down again. And Mark showed that he could outrun the big man. Ira was puffing when they stopped.

"I had a long talk with Brother Frankie Vitale tonight, Ira. He sends his condolences."

"What's this Brother shit? Vitale ain't black, he's a wop."

Mark nodded. "And about as stupid as you are. How long did you bastards think you could go on busting up players and getting away with it? Bartholemue is an idiot, you should have known that."

"I don't know what you're saying, man."

Mark hit him in the side of the neck with a sharp, half-power karate chop and moved away from him so quickly that Ira had no time to defend himself or to retaliate.

"Christ, what the hell you doing?"

"Why did you try to kill me in my sleep, you ugly bastard?"

"Got me, smart fuck, why?"

Mark took the silenced .45 from his belt and fired a round between the big black man's spread feet. The guard danced backward, surprise and fear on his face.

"Easy with that thing!"

"Yeah, a guy could get hurt with this. Could even get a knee smashed, and if nobody heard him out here until morning, he could come damn close to bleeding to death."

"Oh, shit. You wouldn't."

"I would."

The big man outweighed Mark with his 260 pounds, but he wasn't as fast. Mark had proved that to him.

"First, I should tell you that Vitale told me it was you who pushed Cully off the balcony. Vitale's going to testify against you. With a good lawyer you could plead manslaughter and be out in, what, four or five years."

"Hey!"

"Average. It could go ten years depending on the jury's recommendations. Now with a confession it might get cut down to two years, if the judge goes along."

"What's all this bullshit? I didn't even *know* Cully. Saw him around practice for two days. That's all."

"That's a damn shame, Ira. Hell. So, it's your knee, you made the choice, not me." Mark lifted the silenced .45 and aimed the long muffler at Ira's right knee.

"No!" Ira's big voice boomed. "No shooting. That way I'm busted up for good, never play ball again." He thought about it. "Somebody's got to convict me first. Shit, I'll take my chances with a jury. I can buy the best lawyer around, and I didn't shove no Cully off no fucking balcony. Where is that asshole Vitale, I'll pound the truth out of him."

Mark told Ira exactly where Vitale was at the moment, and the big black guard sobered.

"You don't fuck around legal, do you? You Mafia for Christ's sakes?"

"No. Now which knee do you want it in, Ira?"

Ira rushed him. He was good and had waited until Mark was slightly off balance and moving. Mark had no chance to avoid him completely. The Penetrator jolted to one side and slammed the heavy silencer downward as he saw one huge black arm swipe at his torso. The silencer bit into flesh just above Ira's wrist and both men could hear the crack as at least one wrist bone broke.

Ira screamed, then choked it off and fell to his knees, holding his wrist.

"You bastard! You no-good fucking bastard!

I'll kill you! I'll tear your damn head off your fucking shoulders!"

Mark kicked him in the kidney hard enough to hurt him but not to double him up.

"Who helped you push Cully over the rail? Whose room did you step into when I came steaming down the far stairs? Talk, Brother, or you'll won't see a doctor until morning and by then you'll be dead."

Ira lay there moaning, holding his wrist, rocking back and forth.

"You got off lucky, Ira. It should have been your knee. I promised Cully it would be both your knees." Mark touched the big black left hand. "I slap that hand around and you'll pass out from the pain, Ira. I wake you up and do it again, and we go through that three or four times. You want that? Nobody is gonna hear you screaming out here this time of night."

"You wouldn't."

Mark slapped the hand below the broken wrist and Ira sucked in a surprised breath and then roared in fury and agony. When his screams quieted down, Mark began again, his voice steady, neutral.

"Now, Ira, did anyone help you push Cully over the rail?"

"No."

"Word came down he was working for the commissioner?"

"Yes. Cully was a danger to us. He had to go."

"Whose room did you go into when I ran by?"

"Vitale's. I was down the steps and into his

room ahead of you. Now take me to the damned doctor!"

"Who do you get your instructions from?"

"I don't know, just a voice on the phone and a code word and then the orders."

"Bart Bartholemue of the Elks. Is he one of the top dogs?"

"Yes, but I don't know how. Now get me to a doctor."

Mark sighed. "A knee would have been one hell of a lot better, Ira." Coach and his doctor could handle this on campus. "Get up, Ronkowski, you have to walk to that phone over by the gym."

At the phone, Mark called Coach Sample's private number. It took longer for Ben to get to the phone this time. Mark told him he had nailed the two Brothers, and named them. The coach swore.

"We'll miss Ronkowski."

Mark told him where Vitale was, but warned the coach to wait until he heard from the police about him. "Ronkowski is easier. Get the team doctor out of bed and you can pass this off as a broken wrist, a hairline fracture from the scrimmage."

Coach Sample swore again. "Proof, we'll need proof."

"Charge both Vitale and Ronkowski with Cully's murder. Vitale will sing like a bird to save his hide from the murder and the double killing of that pair of stiffs he's still holding hands with. I'll call Detective Jones and have him meet us at the dispensary."

14

Up the Ladder

The Penetrator walked a whining Ronkowski past the gym to the small building used as a medical facility and for physical therapy by the camp. Various medical machines had been set up, including a portable X-ray. Mark parked Ronkowski beside the locked door and told him to wait right there until the doctor came.

"Not afraid I'll run off?"

"Not until your wing is patched and by then the cops will have you nailed on murder one."

Mark faded into the night. There was a lot he had to do in a short time. Back in his dorm room he changed his clothes, left most of his gear there, and hurried to his car. He checked his suitcases. Yes, enough of everything. He put them away, and wheeled out of the lot headed back toward the University of California at Irvine, where he had played football that afternoon. Only this time he was not going to play a game; his business was much more serious.

Mark found a state park along the ocean halfway to Irvine and pulled in and slept by the water on a hummock of soft sand with only a light blanket from the car. He was up by daylight, packed and drove up the Interstate to a good breakfast stop. He arrived at the UCI campus just as the first practice sessions were getting underway. No rest for the wicked—or for pro football players.

Security on the field was almost nonexistent. This was a day the public was invited to watch the practices. Mark got on the practice field by saying he had a special message for Coach Bartholemue. One of the guards pointed out the heavyset ex-player who had lost his battle at the table.

Bartholemue worked with the kickers and Mark had no problem walking right up to him.

"Hank, what the hell I got to tell you about your left shoulder. You're a goddamned socker-style kicker, remember? You got to keep your fucking left shoulder even with your right until just *before* you kick the ball. Then you turn your whole body directly at the goalposts. Now try it again."

Bartholemue glanced up at Mark. "Who the hell are you?"

"Just a fan, from San Diego. I have a private message for you."

"From who, hotshot?"

"Guy named Carmine Lavangetti."

"Oh, why the fuck didn't you say so? Over here."

They walked a few yards away from the nearest player.

"Keep on punching them through, Hank. When you do twenty in a row from thirty yards, you tell me."

The coach looked up, his face curious. "What the hell does Carmine have to say?"

"He says it's all over, the two Brothers in San Diego have been busted for murder one, and the whole thing is a washout. He just wanted to warn you in advance."

"I don't believe it, I just don't *believe* it. Look, you stay right here. We got to talk. I'll get these guys moving and then we're gonna have some words in the office." He went over to the kickers, and told another man with a red hat on to work with the kickers. Bartholemue motioned to Mark as he walked past him.

They went into an office, then into a larger room that had been set up as a weight and strength area.

"You heard the news broadcasts yet this morning?"

"No," the Penetrator said.

Bartholemue took a small tape recorder from his desk and punched the play button.

"CCN-TWO sports. The National Football League and the San Diego Sharks were rocked this morning when police reports indicated that two of the starters from the division champions had been arrested and booked on murder charges. They are being held in connection with the death a few days ago of a standout rookie named Cully Ambrose, who fell to his death from a third-floor stairwell on the UCSD campus during the Sharks' annual camp.

"Detective Will Jones, of the San Diego Police, said both men were being held after one implicated the other. They are Ira Ronkowski, starting offensive guard, and pass-snagging wide receiver Frank Vitale. Both are being held without bail. Jones said Ronkowski was picked up while he was being treated for a broken wrist suffered in the Sharks-Elks scrimmage yesterday at Irvine. Vitale had been discovered early this morning handcuffed to two dead men on Torrey Pines State Beach. From police reports Vitale implicated his teammate in the Cully Ambrose death."

When Mark looked back at Bartholemue, the coach was aiming a small-caliber automatic at Mark's chest. He pushed a button on his desk and four big men hurried in through the door.

"This is him, boys, frisk him and be careful, he's a whirlwind with both hands and feet. Up against the wall, Wilson, or whatever your real name is. You know the position, lean in and spread your feet."

One of the big men took Ava and Mark's .45, as well as the stiletto from his boot.

"Fucker was loaded for bear, coach."

"Fine, then we're *sure* who we have here. Lock the doors and don't let anyone in."

Two of the big men grabbed Mark's arms and walked him backward toward the weight machines. They tied his hands to the top of one of the machines and tied twenty-pound weights around his ankles. Then one of the big men slugged Mark in the stomach. Mark knew the blow was coming and tightened his muscles, but it only partly blunted the pain. Then the specialist slapped Mark's face one way and then the other five times. Bartholemue stood in front of Mark.

"Who are you working for, Wilson? The commissioner? You might as well tell us, then we won't have to arrange an accident for you. You don't tell us and you're a dead man."

"I work with Ronkowski. I'm his number one man. All the Brothers have helpers, you know that. Christ, I'm next in line when Ronkowski gets traded or gets blown out of it."

Bartholemue laughed and shook his head. "No way, Wilson. I *know* who those men are in all twenty-eight clubs, and you don't show on any of the lists. Now who the hell do you work for? Did you set up our two boys down there? How did you nail them? How the hell did you get them to testify *against* each other?"

"How? You're kidding. With a couple of morons like those guys, anybody could have done it. You've got to get better people in your organization, Bartholemue."

"When we do, you won't be one of them." He nodded and a new heavyweight came in with thin leather gloves, the kind that boxers use when working on the heavy punching bag. Mark knew the rough stuff was just starting. The boxer wasn't watching Mark's feet and he lifted the twenty-pound weight and shot his foot into the man's belly. The big man grunted, then bellowed in pain and dropped to the floor.

"For that I'll break your goddamn head!" the

ex-jock screamed running at Mark, but Bartholemue stepped in front of him.

"Wait. Let's soak him for a while, at 180 degrees. That will loosen him up."

"That's not even warm for a whirlpool, Bartholemue," Mark said.

"It isn't the whirlpool. You'll see."

They pushed him ahead of them into another room, one that had been double-locked, and Mark saw what it was the university's special experimental isolation/immersion chamber. There were caution signs all around. The room was to be used only by qualified personnel, the chamber was never to be sealed completely, it was to be used upon special authorization only. At no time was the subject to be left alone in the room. A monitor with audio and visual contact had to be functioning well at all times and communication maintained.

"They put me in here for an hour the other day. I almost went out of my skull and asked to be let out. It is absolutely terrifying in there. Should fit you to a T, Wilson, you bastard."

Mark shrugged at Bartholemue. "Doesn't matter, the die is cast. You and your ring are dead. There's only a little mopping up to be done by the Federal Grand Jury. I hope you aren't afraid of small jail cells, Bartholemue."

"I'll never go into the slammer, wise-ass. Now jump in."

They had unlocked and lifted the special entry hatch on the dark chamber. It looked like an oversize bathtub, with a plastic enclosure on top made of heavy material painted black and fastened together on the inside. The cover was barely two feet above the level of the water. The device was eight feet long, with a head-resting cup and minimal floating devices in a kind of sling that gave that ten percent flotation help most people need.

"Hell, don't take your clothes off, they'll help sag you down. You'll go out of your skull in there after a couple of hours." Bartholemue laughed. "Yeah, and after six hours you'll be clawing your eyes out and threshing around and eventually drown yourself. Yeah! Just wish I could be here to look in through the porthole and watch you."

One of the big men pushed Mark forward and he stepped into the tepid water, then shrugged and stretched out in the wetness. They had all his weapons, and they would shoot him at any provocation. The two big men now seemed to be more Mafia soldier types than ex-football players. Mark felt the flotation gear move up as he sank into it, as some kind of electronic brain gauged his weight and adjusted the device to keep him ninety-nine percent submerged. His head fit neatly into the foam-rubber rest and he let his hands float at his sides.

"Take your last look at a living human being, Wilson. You're gonna die in there, and I say good riddance!" Bartholemue slammed the door on the chamber and it was suddenly, powerfully dark.

For a moment Mark didn't breathe. It was a remarkable sensation, the total darkness and nearly total silence. Somewhere he heard a motor start. A pump, he reasoned. At the same time he felt warmer water flowing into the tank from the four edges. There were some muted sounds outside the chamber, then he heard a door close faintly, but after that there was only silence and the steady loudness of his own breathing.

Questions bombarded him. Had they locked the door? He tried it and found they had. Did it have some sort of internal safety device on it? He figured it did; if only he knew how to activate it. What about normal use of the room? Would there be anyone coming in during this part of the day? Were all the regular researchers who used the room off for the summer?

As the dozen questions bounced around in his head, he worked up his *Sho-tu-ca* powers of sight and the blackness faded out to a dull gray. There was almost no natural light to work with, but at last he made out the ridges and seals on the top of the chamber and saw that there was only an inch of freeboard from side to top. Would it leak? He tried making waves with his legs, but couldn't tell if any water seeped out or not.

The water coming in changed from warm to hot, and he judged how long it would take the filtration system to change the tepid water completely into hot and then to near boiling if Bartholemue had his way. Not very damn long!

Mark checked the device again. There was plenty of room for him to hang over the water against the plastic top, if there were some way to hold on. He examined the lower edges of the chamber. His feet could fit there, with his back pressed firmly against the roof, and his hands. . . . Yes, his hands could brace against the interior lumps of metal that had to be the hinges on the door. The old arch technique.

The only question was, how long could his stomach and arm muscles hold him out of the water?

Mark moved into the arch position, using the plastic headrest as his first support, but his hands remained in the water. At anything over 120 degrees that would not be possible.

Using all of his skills as a human fly, Mark worked up the sides of the ceiling inch by inch with his hands, until he reached the lower door hinge. Yes, it would work. He was out of the water, and the strain would not be too bad. He tested the water.

It wasn't hot yet. He let himself back into the wetness and stripped his belt buckle off his two-inch belt. The buckle was heavy brass and had several interesting devices on it, few of which could aid him here. He did extend a folded blade from the side, which would work as a screw-driver, knife, or pry bar. It was three inches long and made of the best tempered steel avail-able.

There were no interior screws. There was noth-ing he could cut. He jammed the blade into the seal between the door and the chamber and to his surprise it penetrated the rubber. Quickly he worked it all the way through and bent it back and forth. Soon he had pried a small hole out of the compressible rubber material that formed the seal. If the blade were outside it might attract attention.

His *Sho-tu-ca*-intensified hearing picked up the sound of a door opening and closing. He wiggled the knife blade, then pulled it back in and pounded the heavy buckle against the plastic interior. The plastic was not like metal, and made only a dull clunking sound that he was afraid wouldn't carry. He clunked on it in series code, then with S.O.S. in Morse code. But nothing happened. Two or three precious minutes later the door opened and closed again and then Mark heard nothing.

The water was getting hotter. He figured he could remain in it for another five, maybe six minutes before he would have to get out.

His bootlaces!

Mark pulled up one of his half boots and unlaced it, lifting the square leather thong out of the water. With the screwdriver point of the blade, he worked the end of the shoelace into the hole he had made and then began pushing it into the hole, threading it through and hoping it would dangle down from the door. With the two-foot length of shoelace outside he would stand a better chance of attracting attention.

The water was much hotter now.

Mark pushed the blade time and time again, then counted twenty more thrusts until he had the lace through and only an inch of it was left inside. He tied that around the blade and waited.

He felt the water warming him, heating through him. It was getting uncomfortable, but he could stand it another five minutes before he lifted out.

He had to wait for someone to come into the room.

As he waited he explored the interior of the chamber around the door hunting for a safety feature, a quick release. With all of the emphasis on safety these days, he thought, there would be something built into this device.

He found nothing, only slippery, sweating plastic, wet, smooth, unyielding plastic.

No one entered the room. He lifted out of the water now and braced himself with one hand, caught the leather thong and the small knife blade and swung it out to lock in place. Then he forced the blade through the seal again, and pressured and powered it to the side, cutting, slicing, tearing the rubber apart. If it had an inch of soft compressible rubber on each side, and it joined together, there would be an inch-long opening between the two members. He ripped and tore, changed hands, holding himself arched over the water with the other hand and tore at the softness of the seal again.

Progress.

But was it fast enough? He was sweating now as the temperature in the vessel rose well past 100 degrees. He had no idea what the water temperature was.

He could see a slash six inches long and a faint light seeping through it.

Faster! Harder!

Work at it or die!

The reality of failure skittered across his mind,

but he drove it away with a fury that surprised him. He worked the knife blade through the opening now, forcing material outside the chamber, tearing the thick rubber away from its seal. Now he could work his fingers outside the lip of the door!

He jammed them through as far as possible with his palm downward, so he could feel for any kind of a catch, latch, or trigger that would open the hatch door. He found nothing.

His support arm slipped and he had to ram his left hand down quickly six inches into the water against the side of the chamber to hold himself out of it. Mark repositioned his dry hand and then pulled his left one out. It was burned, he had felt the skin react to the sudden hot water. Not scalding, but hotter than he could stand without some injury to the flesh.

He shook the hand and arm, then pushed his left fingers through the torn place again, this time with his fingers reaching upward.

He touched something.

Mark pressed forward and extended his hand farther. A small flush kind of device. A pressure button? Yes, a button, but he didn't have enough reach to force the center of it downward!

Quickly he pulled his hand inside and tore at the rubber sealing material with the knife where he had found the button. His right foot slipped and his shoe hit the water before he could jerk it upward. His shoe protected his flesh but there was an uncomfortable heat transferred to the leather. He jerked and tore and pulled at the material around the seal, then thrust his fingers out and upward again.

Close.

Again he tore at the sealing rubber at the top side of the slot, cutting away an inch of it with slow painful strokes with the knife.

His left hand hurt, and he tried to bring his *Sho-tu-ca* powers to it, but he couldn't, he was concentrating so massively on the project at hand.

Once more he pushed his hand, this time his right, through the opening and forced himself to stretch his fingers as far as possible and then brought them in contact with the exterior of the chamber. He found the button.

Mark strained with every muscle in his hand and arm and, his index finger pressed forward, touched the button and pushed it in as hard as he could.

He heard a small, soft click and he released the pressure on the top of the door. The entire panel above his hand moved outward a half inch.

Mark pulled his hand in and pushed the hatch upward.

The hatch lifted!

A gush of steam erupted from the isolation chamber, and Mark gulped in lungfuls of fresh cool air.

He worked his feet around the vessel slowly, then pushed and half dove through the opening. His feet splashed in the near-boiling water, but the boots protected him.

Slowly Mark crawled from the hatch, put his

feet on the floor and sat there leaning against the heavy plastic. He looked at his left hand and wrist. The flesh was pink, with a few blisters, but not as bad as he had feared. He could flex his fingers, move the wrist. First-degree burns were all. He lifted to his feet, stooped and laced in two eyelets on both sides to secure his half boot, and then moved toward the door.

Before he got there he heard a key. He leaped to the side, touched his belt, and found the thin double wire garotte and pulled it free. On each end was an inch-long loop designed to hold a short stick or some other device. He flattened his body against the wall by the hinged side of the door and waited.

It opened and a man walked into the room and closed the door before he looked at the chamber. He was one of the Mafia-style hoods. Just as he turned, Mark slammed him with a *uchi mawashi geri,* an inside roundhouse kick.

His boot landed flush on the point of the big man's chin, and Mark could see his whole body dissolve into unconsciousness as it fell. His eyes blinked out, his arms dropped, then his knees gave up and he hit the floor in a jumbled pile of arms and legs.

Mark looked for a weapon first, found it in his shoulder leather, removed the .45, checked the clip, and worked the lever, charging one round into the firing chamber.

Now he felt more prepared. He searched the other pockets and found one of the Mafia five-dollar gold pieces. It figured.

Mark ran back to the isolation chamber and

closed the hatch again, then dragged the unconscious soldier away from the door and peered out a one-inch slot into the hall. A dozen men moved out there. It must be the lunch break. Mark took off his soaked shirt and exchanged it for the big hoodlum's. No way that the pants would fit. He brushed back his damp hair with his hands and started to check the hallway again. Just before he did, two men came through the door, talking to each other. When the first looked up, Mark had the .45 almost up his nose.

"Inside, and close the door gently," Mark said in a soft voice. One of the men Mark had seen in Bartholemue's office, Mafia, the other one was smaller, and looked frightened of the weapon.

"Hey! Don't point that damn thing at me," the smaller, younger one said.

"You have a weapon on you?" Mark asked him.

The kid shook his head.

"The goon here does. Take it out nice and slow, soldier, hold it by the barrel and lay it gently on the floor." When he did Mark thundered a left-footed kick into his chin, snapping his head backward, and Mark heard the small unusual sound of a broken neck happening.

"God, that could hurt him!" the small man said.

"Not any more, nothing can. You want the same treatment?"

The kid shook his head, his face suddenly chalk white. He turned his head and vomited.

Mark had no idea how many personal bodyguards and Mafia soldiers Bartholemue had brought into the camp for his own needs. It would be better to get out of here as quickly as possible.

"Who are you, son?"

"I'm assistant to the PR director." His eyes were still wide. "Christ, that guy is *dead*."

"As a doornail. Think of him as a rattlesnake who got killed. No great loss. He's a Mafia gangster, do you know that? Before they get their membership card they have to make their bones. In the Family lingo, that means they have to kill someone, preferably an enemy of the family, but not necessarily."

"Jesus. . . ."

"Now, kid, you and me are walking out of here, both alive. You are going to escort me quickly to the far parking lot and then off campus. If anything goes wrong, you are one son-of-a-bitching dead mother's son. You understand?"

"Yes. Who are you?"

"Just a friend who doesn't like Mafia goons in the Elks' organization. Let's go."

15

Blow Away Three

It was a walkaway.

Mark and his escort simply walked out of the room, down the hall and outside, and none of the other men in the area paid any attention to them. The kid from the PR office was scared spitless all the way. At the edge of the farthest parking lot where Mark had left his car they stopped.

"You do want to go on living?" Mark asked.

"Yes . . . yes, sir!"

"How good a memory do you have? If you can forget ever seeing me, forget ever walking into that room and watching that filthy hoodlum die, I might let you go."

"Yes . . . yes. You say that guy was a criminal, a killer?"

"You won't find many Mafia triggermen teaching Sunday school or helping out the Red Cross. They are evidently working with or for one of your assistant coaches, Bartholemue. I don't think any of them will be around much longer. Do me and yourself a big favor, and just sit on this story for a couple of days, okay? It won't take long, it's coming to a head real soon. It's called the Brotherhood of Blood, and they killed Cully Ambrose down at the Shark camp last week."

"God!"

"True. I'm working with the football commissioner's office and we're trying to get it all straightened out. Now, let's see how fast you can run from here back to the practice field and then to the far end."

"Okay, yeah, I can run. Get the bastards, they're trying to ruin football."

"Go, kid."

He ran. When he was past the gym, Mark ran to his rented car, got in, and drove away before the young man could possibly get back to take down his license number.

To Mark it seemed like he was never done, there was always somebody else trying to mess up the American dream, trying to get something for nothing, trying to take what they wanted by force, or deception, instead of working for it.

Mark drove half a mile away, parked near a big college building and got into his emergency suitcase and took out some ointment which he spread over his burned hand. The paw would be good as new in two or three days. Just so he didn't have to go up any four-story vertical walls for a while.

He changed clothes unobtrusively, put on some dark brown slacks and a brown T-shirt with some stripes on it, and drove to a drug store, where he got a pair of large sunglasses with reflective lenses and a L.A. Elks billed cap. He got back to the practice field and sat in the bleachers watching the workout. His hand hurt like hell the rest of the afternoon.

When practice was over, Mark faded into the campus near the dormitories the team used, and trailed Coach Bartholemue when he left the coaches' offices. He only had two goons with him this time and he looked carefully along his path.

Mark stayed well to one side and saw Bartholemue go into one of a series of individual residences about a block from the dorms.

It seemed he was the only one living there. The two watchdogs settled down, one on the front porch and, Mark guessed, the other one in the rear.

Mark waited and watched. Just after eight that evening, a car pulled up in the street in front and two men left it and went up to the porch. The guard welcomed them and let them inside.

Mark checked the rear of the house and found a guard there. The Penetrator took a long, rod-like device from one of his pockets and screwed it on the barrel of his .45 and worked his way slowly toward the guard who was reading the sports pages of the *Los Angeles Times* and listening to a radio broadcast.

Mark was ten feet away when the gangster looked up. Mark's big .45 automatic with the silencer coughed once and the Mafia torpedo grew a new eye in the middle of his forehead as the heavy slug bored into his brain, slowed due to the sound supressor, and shattered on its way through the upper lobe, tearing vital nerve cen-ters into masses of useless, tangled commo wire, empty sockets, and uncompleted messages.

The guard jolted backward four feet and fell with the newspaper still clutched in his dead hands.

Mark left the hood where he lay, tested the back door and found it unlocked, and eased inside, closing the panel behind him.

He was in a kitchen, small, carefully decor-ated by a cheerful, artistic person.

Voices came from the other room. Mark saw steps leading upward. He crossed the eatery and found the steps blocked off from view of the living room and took them two at a silent time to check out the high ground.

No one was in any of the three bedrooms upstairs, although two of them had been used. He saw nothing to help or hinder and moved back toward the hall. Mark found a small over-look area that opened onto the living room from the short hall, and with a quick look he saw the men grouped below.

An ordinary but familiar voice held the floor.

"Sure, we're in trouble with the Sharks. We have two choices, either we silence the two Brothers, or we dump them. No other options. I'll report in tomorrow night. As for this oper-ation, and the rest of us, the decision is we hang tough and see what happens in San Diego."

Mark eased up to the edge at floor level and looked through the small balcony railing. Coach

Bartholemue was there and two men Mark had never seen before, neither of whom could be confused with an ex-pro football player.

Another voice chipped in.

"We've got a lot of work to do to set up the season. We've got to guess which team is going to come alive, which ones will do best. We can't have a big upset every week or pretty soon the betters are going to get wise. But just using our two Brotherhood players, we usually can swing a game. Hell, we'll keep working the first half like last year. If we don't have the control we want, we put the hammer down and start taking out the other team's key players any way we can. A few words from the Brothers on one team to the Brothers on the other can do wonders, too."

The smaller of the two nodded. "Yeah, right, but we need to look for more tight ends and wide receivers now when we need to replace. They can be game breakers or game losers. And this can mean big, big money. We get a good tight match set up and put the odds at, say, two to one against the underdog, we can put down a million bet at one club alone and clean up."

Bartholemue spoke up. "The Brothers are asking for a bigger cut. They say for the risk they take of being exposed, the hundred thousand a year is chicken feed."

"To us that's a six-million-dollar payroll. We've got big expenses. But you tell the network that we'll see what we can do for them. First let's get the season rolling. We can't do anything in the preseason games, because most betters don't look at them as contests, they are exhibitions, and the damn coaches play everybody to see what they can do under game conditions.

"Oh, we will need to do some quick recruitment in San Diego. What about the number two team down there, are they ready and willing to move up?"

Bartholemue shook his head. "No way. Not either one of them. Sparky is tainted now, and I don't like the other one. Things are going to be sticky down there for a couple of months."

"We need control of the Shark's games. They will be a big draw on the betting book. Get something set up before the opener. That's your job, Bartholemue. Carmine would be pissed if you let us down on this one.

"Now, what the hell happened this morning? You said you had this Penetrator character dead and delivered."

"I can't figure it, Pete. There was no way he could get out of there. From what we can put together, he had some kind of a tool with him, a knife, and he sawed through the rubber seals and got the door open, then evidently Rocco came in on him and the bastard broke Rocco's neck. We had to get Rocco out of there and fake a car crash. Now who the hell knows where this Penetrator is. He gave the Family a bad time a few years back, but we haven't seen much of him lately. He's twice as tough and twice as mean as I figured he'd be. He's a real deadly fucking bastard!"

"I'll have to tell Carmine when I see him

tomorrow. He's gonna really be pissed. He figured we had that one million head money. Even a don will go out of his way for that kind of change."

"Hell, the guy is a magician."

"Nobody can dodge a .45 round from a foot away. That's how I'll handle the big sonofabitch if I ever face him. Nothing fancy, just one slug in the back of the head and he's mine."

"Next time," Bartholemue said. "Now let's get down to it. We need one new man in Cincinnati where Jones retired, and we need the two new ones in San Diego. We have rosters?"

The men spread out papers on a coffee table and grouped around them. Mark wished he had a fragger, what a beautiful target. But he didn't want to smash up the university's house. The trio hadn't noticed the rear guard was down yet. Mark would have to move soon before they did. But he wanted to learn as much about the operation as he could before he hit them.

San Diego was cleaned out. But he couldn't go from town to town working on each team. The head, chop off the top men and the rest of it would wither. He had been right about that. And it looked like he had three of the top men right below him.

"It's going to take some money and some cultivation in San Diego, especially if we go to a pair of new men," Bartholemue said.

"Hell, a few parties, two girls per man, and a few snorts of coke will do wonders. Bart, you used to be one of them. You know how they think, what's important: good women, good booze, good coke. Hell, you won't have any trouble on that score."

"I hope to hell not. It's gonna be touchy down there."

The Penetrator did not believe in the code of the Old West, or in the bromide of giving a killer a fair chance. When he had a target, and that man had been confirmed as Mafia or other scum that needed to be exterminated, he simply exterminated. The Penetrator liked the high ground. He leveled the .45 and its bulky silencer across the carpet of the balcony floor and aimed in on the smallest of the three men who seemed to be next-in-command to Carmine Lavangetti in Las Vegas. He refined his sights and put the first round through the left side of hoodlum's face just above his ear.

The cough of the silenced .45 sounded loud in the room and the heavy slug slamming into the skull could have been someone thumping a melon for ripeness. Then all similarities ended as the Mafia man slammed away from the coffee table as the slug spilled him half over the sofa with his head almost touching the floor, and half his skull blown off with brains, tissue, and blood streaming onto the beige university carpet.

The reaction of the other two men was immediate. The second Mafia soldier dove behind the same sofa before Mark could sight in on him. Bartholemue seemed frozen in place for a moment, then he clawed for a weapon as he rolled to one side. Mark's second round ground through his left arm and then he was out of sight below the balcony. A shot whispered past Mark, chipping the wooden balcony support. Mark put three rounds through the near end of the sofa, then pulled back and went down the stairs quickly but silently on the well-carpeted treads, the .45 in one hand and Ava with her deadly red-tipped darts in the other. The air-powered gun held six of the darts ready for reasonably fast fire.

Around the corner of the stairwell he could see most of the living room. The dead man's feet and torso showed on the front of the sofa. Bartholemue had left or was hiding somewhere. An arm lay behind the sofa. Slowly a head edged forward, still looking at the balcony. Mark sighted in, now holding the big .45 with both hands. When the Mafia hoodlum's head was fully visible and his gun hand in sight as well, Mark spoke to him.

"Over here, asshole."

The man jerked his head around, his eyes staring at the muzzle of the .45 as Mark fired. Suddenly the whole side of the hoodlum's head exploded away from him as the .45 round ripped into his forehead, slanting down and outward, tearing off a big chunk of skull and tissue as it snuffed out the lights on the Vegas gambler's last roll.

Mark looked left, exposed himself near the floor to see the rest of the living room. Then a door slammed. Mark dashed around the wall into the kitchen, then, seeing no one there, darted to the back door and kicked it open. He saw

Bartholemue streaking past the dead man in the chair and into a woodsy, brush-filled "privacy strip" behind the house.

The Penetrator jolted from one bit of cover to another, working out the back door, past a parked car, then into the brush and behind a large tree. He stopped and listened.

Something crashed ahead and to the left. Mark moved that way silently.

It was a game of cat and mouse, but the cat in this case was talented, experienced, and skilled in jungle warfare. A walk through the woods became child's play for him.

Bartholemue blundered ahead, smashing down brush, breaking dry sticks on the ground, kicking dead leaves, leaving both a visual and very audible trail for Mark to follow.

Quickly Mark closed the distance until he could see the man ahead. He paused at the edge of the artificial woodsy area, and then ran flat out for the ravine that sank away from the campus toward the desert-type native growth in the arroyo below.

The Penetrator thought of taking the silencer off his .45 to give it its normal range, but knew the sound of the shot would bring campus police. He left the heavy device in place and angled down hill from where his quarry entered the head-high brush. He stopped behind some growth and listened. Even without his accented hearing he could hear the man running. Mark picked the side of the ravine where the brush was thinner, whipping aside the sagebrush and the greasewood and running quickly. He got to a point he thought would be ahead of Bartholemue and stopped, quieted his breathing, and listened.

Yes, the sound came from behind, moving downhill toward Mark.

The Penetrator found a heavy stand of thick growth he didn't know the name of and waited, totally shielded from the man running wildly downhill.

Mark watched Bartholemue coming. At the last moment the Penetrator jumped out in front of the big man, the silenced .45 aimed at his heart.

"Hold it!" Mark barked.

Bartholemue's anger melted into fear. He dropped to his knees as much in exhaustion as fear. The small automatic in his hand fell to the ground, and he looked up at Mark with wild eyes and held his wounded left arm.

"Go ahead, shoot me. What the hell are you waiting for? You already killed three good men and ran off the other one. Just who the hell *are* you anyway, Penetrator?"

"I'm just a private citizen who doesn't like to see a gang of mobsters running things. And I like my sports with at least some semblance of chance involved in who wins." Mark started to pull the trigger, but changed his mind.

"Stand up." Mark ordered.

Bartholemue heaved to his feet.

"Now strip, I want to be sure you don't have any other weapons. Take them off. You're going to have to go on living a while. I want you in the courts. I'll turn over enough evidence on you to keep the Orange County district attorney questioning you for a year. You'll be up on so many charges no one will believe it."

Bartholemue took off his shirt and pants and stopped.

"Come on, fat ass, all the way, give the campus girls a thrill. I'll be behind you going back to your quarters. You won't see me, but I'll be there. Now, march up the hill, and think about all the good football players you had busted up for a few goddamed dollars!"

Mark hounded him up the brush-choked gully to the edge of the campus, then stayed in the concealment while Bartholemue began his naked dash from tree to tree across the campus toward his temporary residence. Halfway across, two college boys saw him. One of them gave him a light windbreaker which he tied around his waist as he ran on toward his body-filled house.

Mark came out of the brush, hid his weapon, and jogged around the street to his car.

He watched all around him but saw no movement. A moment later he heard sirens and edged his vehicle away from the curb and headed for the airport. He needed to catch a quick flight to Las Vegas, somebody should be flying there. Part way up the freeway toward Los Angeles International Airport he changed his mind. He wouldn't be able to take enough of his weapons on the plane, he'd drive. It wasn't that far. He settled in on the freeway and kicked the accelerator, bringing the rented rig up to seventy miles an hour. The cops probably wouldn't bother him. If they did, he had a valid driver's license. Las Vegas, sin city. Get ready, Carmine, you and your crew are going to have a visitor soon, a visitor with a fist full of death!

16

Skimming A Las Vegas Family

As Mark drove toward Las Vegas through the maze of Los Angeles freeways, he thought about the "Robin Hood" tag some writers and many of those he had helped along the way had given to him. A few newspaper writers were frankly pleased with the way he cut through official rules and red tape of justice and dealt with problems the local police didn't seem to want to confront or couldn't handle.

Justice at the end of a .45-caliber bullet.

But it worked. It was damned effective, and in all his years of missions he had never attacked a law-enforcement man. He had held fast to the idea that each American is worthwhile and precious and if he couldn't stand up for his rights, then Mark would do the job for him. The very idea that gangsters and politicians, and shyster lawyers and mobsters and the Mafia would conspire to cheat, defraud, and rob the people of this country was infuriating to Mark Hardin. He would go on battling them for as long as he could breathe and pull a trigger.

Yes, he killed. But he killed only those who, in his judgement, deserved it, and who were working against the best interests of our society. The honest, hardworking American, whether he was a mechanic, stockbroker, field-worker, farmer, or university professor, had absolutely nothing to fear from the Penetrator. But quite without trying to, the Penetrator had become a focal point for many of the people who thought we had as a nation grown too soft on crime and corruption, closed our eyes to lawbreaking, taken to mob and "gang" rule where the inner city's fastest gun and strongest fist made right.

The Penetrator knew it wasn't so.

The Penetrator would prove it to anyone.

He wound along the freeways through San Bernardino and out across the hills into the deserts around Barstow, and then made the long run to the Nevada border and the "sin city" of Las Vegas. He hung the speedometer at sixty-five miles an hour when there was lots of traffic and California Highway Patrol cars, then opened it up to ninety miles an hour when traffic dropped off and the desert road stretched straight and flat ahead of him.

He arrived at glitter city just as the sun was sliding into the desert behind him, asked directions, and soon was cruising past the Paradise Shores Hotel and Casino. The home of Carmine Lavangetti.

Mark drove past, came back and parked in the big lot in front of the massive ten-story hotel with two wings and the sign that advertised four Hollywood star headliners in the various showrooms and theatrelike halls. The mob had put a lot of money into this one, and Carmine was holding the purse strings. At least that was the word. The Las Vegas family, even under Carmine's father, never put together the kind of money it took to build a layout like this.

Mark began wandering through the casino, played some slots, watched the crap shooters and the blackjack tables. It was easy to spot the pit bosses, the muscle, the floating "persuaders" who could at once get rid of any rowdy, boisterous, or falling-down-drunk customer who was probably broke anyway.

Mark had changed into a dark blue suit with light blue pin-striped shirt and a plain white tie. He had slicked back his hair to make it a little less full. He even *looked* like a hood. He sized up one of the musclemen and took the five-dollar gold piece with the words on it and began flipping it in the air as he stood in front of a man who had to be a soldier.

"Hey, man, I'm lost again. I'll never remember where everything is in this fucking place. I got in from Detroit yesterday and they said just hang around, get acquainted. Hell, I can't even find dinner."

The soldier grinned. "Not that tough, but takes a couple of days. You in a six-man room?"

"Yeah, I guess. You people stay up all goddamned night?"

"Half of us do. That's the way we work. Look, remember this. The next guy you flash that coin at might not be so understanding. Your room is on the second subfloor, that's B. Get to it at the elevators by the kitchen marked "employees only." The bosses are on the tenth floor. Who did you report to, Tassily?"

Mark scratched his head. "Don't sound right?"

"Christ, where do they dig up you guys? Was it Giamba?"

"Yeah, yeah, sounds like it."

"He's the security boss. He's on the ground floor, and his office is just off the entrance, behind those banks of slots. You better keep in touch with him or your ass will be burning."

"Yeah, man, thanks. I got it now. Giamba. Security. I ain't on for four hours yet."

"So enjoy."

Mark moved on. He would take the direct approach. Mark got on the hotel side elevators and went up to the ninth floor, got off, and checked the stairwells. The doors would open from either side. A moment later he had cracked the stair door on the tenth floor and looked down the long hall. Halfway down in front of the elevators sat a receptionist. She was dark and had a great figure and a slinky, low-cut dress. Behind her at a desk by a console sat the biggest telephone operator Mark had ever seen. He also had a bulge under his left armpit, a .38 at least, and probably a scaled-down .45. Mark slid the door closed and went back to the ninth floor elevator. He went to the tenth, got off, and grinned at the girl. He was flipping the gold coin. He stared at the brunette and winked. She ignored him.

"Jesus, just trying to be friendly." Mark noticed that the soldier had checked him out quickly, saw the coin, and relaxed.

Mark leaned on the desk in front of the mafioso. "What the hell's the matter with her? Just trying to be friendly."

"Forget it. What are you doing up here?"

"Damned if I know. Giamba told me to come up and report to Don Lavangetti."

"Why?"

Mark shrugged. "Who knows? A week ago I was in New York, now I'm here on loan. Who knows what the capos are planning."

"I'll check."

He talked on a phone for a moment so Mark couldn't hear.

"Don Lavangetti is busy right now, but the house boss, Palmieri, will talk to you. He thinks there's a mistake somewhere."

Mark shrugged. "Que sera, sera."

"True. End of the hall, last door on the left, then straight ahead."

"Yeah, keep it up," Mark grinned as the hood glanced quickly at the girl. He walked down the hall with just enough swagger. He had worn the suitcoat that allowed room for the .45 under his arm and Ava on his right hip. He had to be careful with his coattails, but everything was covered.

Mark went through the door and straight ahead to a suspicious-looking, baldheaded, pure Italian, who was slightly paunchy, with fringes of hair around the sides of his face, glasses of the older style, dark two-piece suit with the fly zipper showing an inch. A cigar clamped in his mouth had burned out, and his eyes watered as he stared at Mark.

"Who the fuck are you? Giamba almost never sends anyone up to see Don Lavangetti."

"Jesus! I wish you fuckheads out here would get your signals straight. So I'm from New York and don't understand your shitty ways, at least get things straightened out." Mark had waved his hands around as he talked, even turning a little. When he spun back he had the .45 an inch from Palmieri's nose.

"Back up away from the desk, slowly, or you're dead. Now!"

The house boss did as he was told. He looked harmless, like somebody's grandfather, but Mark knew he must have killed fifteen to twenty men to get to the position he held.

"Carmine, where is he?"

Palmieri shook his head.

"Old man, you have five seconds to tell me or you're a dead man pushing up rocks in the cemetery, capish?"

The Mafia house boss sighed. "Carmine is in his office, two doors down, with two men, all well armed. You won't stand a chance of getting out. You might get in. There's a double lock on the door. It works only from the inside."

"Good, I like the challenge. Face the wall and lean in, then spread your legs. You move a muscle and I'll kick you so hard in the balls you'll be eating them for breakfast."

Palmieri moved into the position, Mark took a .38 from his shoulder and stuffed it in his own belt, then took out the silencer for his .45 and screwed it on.

"Now, Palmieri, we're going in to see the big man, and any problems, any tricks, any code words, and you're a dead man, understand?"

"Yes. It's a very good likeness."

"What?"

"The folder Angie sent around on you. The Penetrator. Nobody else would have the guts to come in here this way."

"But, as you said, coming in is easy, getting out is the problem. That's why you live as long as I do inside here, and when you and I get outside in a car moving away with no pursuit, you get the gift of life."

"But. . . ."

Mark waved the silenced weapon at him. "Move it, let's go see the big man himself. Only two inside with him? It will be a small funeral after all."

Palmieri nodded and walked ahead, careful not to make any sudden moves. The door looked like the rest, but had a button and an intercom on the door.

"Say to him, 'Don Lavangetti, I must see you now'."

Palmieri's face sagged in frustration. He would not be able to use the coded messages they had worked out. He would have to do as he was told. No one else moved in the hallway.

Palmieri pushed the button on the device and gave the line as Mark had said it.

The response was immediate.

"What the hell, Palmieri, can't it wait? This is fucking important."

Mark whispered to him. "This is even more important. I feel it is urgent!"

The house boss said the line as indicated and there was a grumbling over the mike. Then it cut off and Mark positioned Palmieri in front of the door and stood by the side. As soon as the lock clicked and the door began to open Mark slammed his shoulder into the older man, jamming him into the door and the door into the man who opened it. Mark came slashing in behind them with both guns out.

"Lace your hands on top of your heads. Now, or you're dead!" Mark barked.

The man who had opened the door sat on the floor, Palmieri had dropped to one knee. Two men stood behind a fancy desk. All did as they were told.

"Palmieri, close the door quietly, then lie on the floor on your face. Don't anyone go for a piece or you're dead."

As he said it the man on the floor rolled and came up with a .38. Mark slammed a .45 hot messenger through the soldier's throat, the silent chuff sounding obscene in the office. His weapons both swung to the pair behind the desk.

"Next?"

The younger man shook his head. "So, you're the Penetrator. Guts, you've got guts, I'll give you that. Right here in my own goddamned office!"

"Silence!" Mark hissed and went to check the desk. The communication box switch was in the "on" position. He snapped it off and carefully took weapons from the hoodlum near the desk, then put him face down on the floor.

Mark stared at Carmine Lavangetti. He was under thirty, darkly good looking, carefully dressed. Then Mark noticed for the first time the twin briefcases on the desk. Both were open, both contained stacks of used bills held together by rubber bands.

"A little early in the day for taking the skim off the top, isn't it, Carmine?"

The young man shrugged.

"The list, Carmine. I want the complete roster of the Brotherhood of Blood. I want the contact man in every team, and any overhead people you have, like Bartholemue."

Carmine laughed.

Mark shot him in the left shoulder with the .45. The Mafia boss spun backwards, bounced off the wall, but remained on his feet.

The soldier on the floor roared and charged Mark. The Penetrator shot him with Ava, and the hood fell four feet short of his goal with a silent whisper of death.

Carmine stared at the Penetrator, agony etched on his face, tears streaming down his cheeks.

"For God's sakes, man. I'll get the damned papers!"

"All of them, Carmine. I wouldn't want to have to put one slug through your balls to encourage you."

"Christ, why can't I hire soldiers like you?" The young man waved at Palmieri to help him and went to a set of file cabinets built into the wall, opened a locked one and took out a folder. The older man took it to the Penetrator.

Quickly he checked it. Yes, names, dates, teams, the complete roster of the Brothers.

Mark nodded, then put the list on the one attaché case filled with money and put Ava away. He closed the case with the money and the file folder inside.

"Palmieri, wrap up that shoulder. Take off his coat, and stop the bleeding. Then the three of us are going for a walk."

It took Palmieri five minutes to stop the blood and bandage Carmine's shoulder. The old man had been around a lot of gunshot wounds. When Carmine got his coat back on his face was pale, and he was gritting his teeth.

"Don Lavangetti isn't feeling well. We'll need his car at his private entrance below. House boss, you give the orders now by phone. No tricks or you're both dead, right here."

Mark watched as the house boss did the job.

"Now, quickly to the private elevator. Is it in this room or the next one?"

Lavangetti pointed to a pair of doors, which Palmieri swung out and opened the small elevator.

"No tricks, and we all live to a ripe old age," Mark said.

The car had only two stop indicators: ten and subfloor one, the garage. When they stopped the door opened automatically. Mark held the attaché case in his left hand and put it around Lavangetti as if helping him. He also held the .45 under his coat with the silencer removed.

When the door slid open a soldier stood there expectantly.

"Fool, get the car door open, Don Lavangetti is ill, we got to get him to the hospital fast," Mark screamed. "Move it, goddamnit!"

The soldier ran to the car. Mark motioned Palmieri into the front seat, helped Lavangetti in the back, and then had him slide over and stepped in beside him.

"Roll it!" Mark shouted, and as soon as the door closed the big Lincoln moved up the ramp to the street. There was no glass shield between front and back.

Mark leaned over and pressed the .45 muzzle into the driver's neck.

"Hand your weapon over your shoulder carefully or this cannon is liable to go off, driver."

The surprised soldier did as he was told.

Mark looked back as they hit the street and flowed into traffic. Another Lincoln came out of the drive after them, a big crew wagon.

"We're being followed!" Mark thundered.

Palmieri nodded. "Normal procedure, the Don doesn't go anywhere with just one car."

"How many men in it?"

"Usually four."

"Use your radio and tell them to return to the hotel."

"They won't without the special orders given by Carmine Lavangetti, personally. They know his voice." Palmieri nodded toward the back seat. "And the Don has just passed out. We can't turn the other car back."

Mark frowned. "Tell them to lead the way to

the best local hospital, the one you always use. Tell them to clear traffic for us."

The house boss hesitated.

"Do it now!" Mark snapped.

Palmieri picked up a mike from the dash and gave the orders. At once the other car whipped around then and blasted ahead. Mark watched them and when the rig came to a section of a limited access street, he made his move.

"Take the turnoff here!" Mark bellowed.

The driver hit the brakes, turned right, skidded, saved it, and then was off the main route into a street of small businesses mixed with houses. Mark watched behind them and saw another car make the turn and follow them. Mark pointed behind them and Palmieri nodded.

"That's Giamba, head of security. He knew something was wrong." It was Palmieri talking.

"Take us out of town, the fastest way, a back road, no highway. Move it, driver, or you're a dead man and just don't know it yet."

The driver behind them stayed with the turns and surges of power, and ten minutes later they snaked down a long, dusty road into the edge of the desert. Nothing grew on either side of the road. A barren yard showed here and there beside an unpainted shack.

The blue car was still with them.

"Slow to ten miles an hour," Mark ordered. The driver did.

"Now turn it crossways in the road and stop. All of you stay exactly where you are." As soon as the car stopped, Mark dove across the unconscious Carmine and out the door away from the oncoming blue car.

When the driver of the other rig saw through the dust and early darkness that the road was blocked, his car was within easy pistol range, and Mark send two rounds from the .45 through the windshield and another one into the radiator. He heard a scream of pain followed by a hissing of steam from the radiator.

One dead blue car.

Mark waited.

The car doors away from him on the blue car opened, and a shot came under the Lincoln near the front wheels where Mark had crouched. He pulled two small devices that looked like cherry bombs from his pocket. Each was three inches long, three-quarters of an inch in diameter, and had a simple burning fuse. Mark fired one of the fuses with a Bic lighter from his pocket and threw the small bomb at the blue car. It skittered under the frame just as it exploded.

It wasn't a cherry bomb.

The special device was a mix of plastique C-4 and gunpowder, with enough of the first to set off the second. The equivalent punch was equal to three sticks of dynamite. The blast jolted the car two feet off the roadway and dropped it back still on its wheels. By the time the explosion had echoed away into the distant hills, Mark had lit and thrown the second C-4 cherry bomb. It landed on the hood and went off at once, blasting the metal hood off the car, and igniting the gasoline spilling from the riddled carburetor. Twenty seconds later the gasoline tank exploded and the car was one huge funeral pyre that lit up the dark sky.

Mark slid back into the car and nudged the driver with his .45. "Drive, on into the desert. Now, son."

When they were another two miles deeper into the desert along the road that had faded into a double row of car tracks, Mark had the driver stop.

"Everyone out," Mark said. He went out on the driver's side and watched the big man as he emerged. Mark had made no search of him and figured he might have a second weapon just waiting for the right time to use it.

The driver came out slowly, then ducked and dove to the ground as he reached for his ankle and a hideout knife. He had it out and threw, but Mark dodged it and was waiting for him. The Penetrator's hot-load .45 caught the driver on the chin, moved upward, and slammed through his mouth and out the top of his head.

Palmieri tried. He came up with a handful of sand that he threw at Mark's eyes with one hand and a baseball-sized rock he threw with the other.

Mark turned the .45 and blasted a round through the house boss's chest, then pounded one more into his open mouth as he screamed.

Mark went back to look at Carmine. He was conscious.

The young Mafia boss stared at him from pain-filled eyes.

"You sonofabitch! You're blowing away my men."

"You didn't make it either, Don Lavangetti. Strange, that I'm the last one to call you by your title."

"We can deal, Penetrator. All the money you want. I'll swear I nailed you in the fire and get the head money. You can go to Mexico City or Toronto and live like a king."

"I live like I want to now, Carmine. I'm doing exactly what I want to do, blasting apart little kingdoms like yours and anybody else in this country or around the world who puts themselves above the law."

Behind them Mark saw a chopper hovering over the burning hulk of the security boss's car.

"Everyone has a price."

"You've been used to buying your way into everything for so long you can't remember what it's like to work for something, Carmine. If it wasn't for the skim you'd be in big trouble. Is it skim just from the state, or are you shorting the Organization?"

Carmine smiled briefly. "Nobody doublecrosses la Cosa Nostra and lives for long. Come on, Penetrator, you must want something. What's your price?"

"I do have a price, Lavangetti."

A smile blossomed over the smaller man's sharp features and he nodded. "Good, whatever it is I'll meet it. Now let's get this crate turned around and go back to town. It's still hot out here."

It's just after dark, Carmine. It'll start to cool off now."

"Not in Las Vegas, tourist, let's go."

"You haven't given me my price yet, Carmine."

"Look, I said I'd pay it, now get me to a doctor before I fucking bleed to death!"

There was a snap and a tone of command in the Mafia don's voice again.

Mark smiled. "First the price. What I want from you, Carmine Lavangetti, is payment for the life of Cully Ambrose. You remember him, he was a football player you had murdered. How much is a life worth, Carmine? For Cully, and for all of the other pro football players you have had broken up and for whom a year has been lost or a career ruined, just so you could make a few dirty dollars, I want your life!"

"Carmine, I want your head on a platter, just like you were going to do to me. My price to you is your life!"

The Mafia don looked at him. There was a new sadness in his face as he realized the man was serious, eternally serious.

"My God!" He stared at Mark. "Nothing is worth such a high price, Penetrator."

"Tell that to Cully Ambrose, or your driver, or to your house boss there with his head blown open. Tell that to all of the men you've killed in the past five years!"

Carmine was sobbing, tears gushed, he reached out a hand.

"For Christ's sakes, Penetrator, make another deal with me!"

"You said you'd give me anything I wanted, this I want. Don't make it harder on yourself by begging."

Carmine tried to silence his weeping.

"Out of the car, Carmine."

The Mafia boss refused.

Mark opened the door, then slowly changed magazines in his .45. When the fresh loads were in the handle, Mark lifted the big .45 and shot the Mafia don twice in the heart with the 185-grain hollow-point slug. He slumped over and Mark put one more round into the side of Carmine's head.

Mark dumped the body out of the car and drove the big Lincoln. He found a connecting track a half mile ahead that wound back towards town, and took it. Twenty minutes later he picked up his rental car at the hotel parking lot, left the floating barrel of his .45 automatic in the limousine, took the attaché case of money and papers and drove to a small motel far out on the edge of town. There wasn't even one slot machine in the little office. What he needed now was a good night's sleep.

Before he went to bed Mark opened the case and looked over the papers again. Yes, everything the commissioner would need. The Brotherhood of Blood was through.

He glanced at the money. Mostly fifties and hundreds, a few stacks of twenties. He would count it later. He guessed there was about a quarter of a million in the case. He knew where it could be put to good use.

17

Maybe A Pickup Game?

Late the next afternoon Mark Hardin parked on campus and went to Coach Ben Sample's office. He carried the file folder in one hand as if it were a trifle. Practice was just over and six coaches crowded into the head man's room for their regular critique, bull session, and exchange of ideas. Mark listened, fascinated by the inner workings of a pro team. One or two of the red-hatted coaches looked at Mark curiously. Ben shut things off early, and told them he'd see them all that evening. They left.

Mark stretched out on the soft sofa and nodded. "Sounds like you're putting together a team. Not too many holes from last year. If you can get those new defensive backs working. . . ."

Coach Sample was on his feet about to explode.

"Damnit, Wilson, what the hell's happened? You've been gone two days. We got our two men locked up on murder one charges, and then you vanish. Give!"

Mark grinned. "It's all over, coach, the Brotherhood just ran out of blood. This file folder is courtesy of the late Don Carmine Lavangetti, of Las Vegas. He gave it to me personally. Read and enjoy." Mark got up to leave.

"Hold it, hold it. Let me see what's in here, and then I need some advice."

The coach began looking over the papers, and he grinned, chuckled, then stared in amazement at some of the names on the list.

"Christ, look at this roster. Fifty-six and some of them are all-pro. This is going to be a damned bombshell. Christ, him? Why, he's got all the money he needs, and three Super Bowl rings." The coach shook his head and reached for the phone. He dialed a number and let it ring.

"Commissioner, this is Ben Sample. Are you having dinner, are you busy?"

He listened for a minute. "Yes, I understand. Well, it's all over, Commissioner. Wrapped up. We've got the complete roster of the Brothers of Blood, the overhead operators, the Mafia tie through Las Vegas has been cut and eliminated. I think you should fly out here tomorrow and take control of this material."

He waved at Mark and listened. "Right, I couldn't agree more, a lifetime banishment from the game in any league. That is mandatory if we can't do anything against the individuals legally, and that would be tough. Deny them the chance to play the game again and it will kill some of them." He paused. "Yes, tomorrow or the next day. Right, we'll see you at the airport if you let us know when you're coming in."

Ben Sample hung up the phone. "So, it's coming down. The commissioner would like to keep it quiet if we can, but I don't see how. With fifty four players banished, no, fifty six counting our two, it will be impossible to keep it quiet. This season is going to have a black mark on it forever. But I'm glad it's cleared up."

He stood and walked around the room, picked up a game ball off his desk and slapped it as he walked. "No other way. They have to be cut off the squads and prevented from playing in the USA League or the Canadian Football League."

"Where are you going to keep that file?" Mark asked.

"I don't know," the coach said.

"Are you sure of all your coaches? Bart Bartholemue of the Elks is in the Brotherhood on a supervisory level, including recruitment."

"God, Bart?"

"Put that file in a safe place."

"I'll bury it deep in the university administration somewhere." The coach stopped. "Oh, yeah, that detective wanted you to call him. Something about testifying."

Mark laughed. "I'll call. Now I've got to get ready to do some fishing."

"The commissioner said he wanted to meet you, to thank you, so hang around a few days."

"Does this mean I have to turn in my pads, that I'm off the team?"

"Hey, Wilson. You can play tight end for me any Sunday you want to suit up, league or exhibition. I owe you. The whole damn league owes you. If you want to hang around and get your body black-and-blue, hell, I'll hold a roster spot open all season."

Mark laughed. "Damn tempting, but I'm not good enough, you know that, coach. Besides, I've got a date to go fishing." He waved and slipped out the door, feeling better than he had in several days.

Mark found the closest phone booth and dialed Marsha Day's number. He let it ring five times, then ten. She was probably out for a while.

He used the same dime and called the detective's number. The sergeant himself picked it up on the third ring.

"Jones."

"Wilson."

There was a pause. "Hey, you've been wandering around on me. I've got to know something. Did you see either of our suspects push Cully off that balcony?"

"Damn right. But I can't help you. He was a shadow, a blur, a shape. It was one of them, but I couldn't swear which one."

"Damn lot of help, Wilson. We've got some of it, the Brotherhood thing, and accusations from both of them charging the other one with the killing. We need something else."

"You'll get it. In a day or two a scandal is going to break that will affect the case. The other players will think hard to come up with what they know. One of them had witnesses, was with three or four other guys when Cully went over. Work that angle. Plea it down, maybe a fight. Neither of those guys is ever going to play pro ball again."

"Good. Now, there is one other thing. Hell! Look, I need a drink, where can I meet you?"

"I was trying to call Marsha. How about tomorrow?"

"No, right now! That bar at the Holiday Inn out there off Ardath Road?"

"Yeah, all right. Half an hour?"

"Done."

Mark stared at the phone, then hung up. He tried to call Marsha again fifteen minutes later' and got no response, so he drove to the motel and went into the bar.

Detective Jones met Mark almost at the door. He didn't have a drink in his hand.

"Good, I thought I missed you, I've got a booth back here. What are you drinking?"

"First, what is bothering you so much you couldn't tell me on the phone?"

"It's bad, Wilson, bad. I'm not good at this sort of thing, though God knows I've done it often enough. I'll just have to say it." They both sat down.

"Wilson, somebody gunned down Marsha Day this afternoon. She's dead."

Mark stared at the SDPD detective.

"Dead?" The shock of it flowed over him like a shroud. His fingers gripped the edge of the booth. He remembered her soft face, the way she had come to the practice field after Cully died, just because she was sorry. He remembered her kind voice on the telephone, how she had promised to take him fishing. Mark took three deep breaths, shook his head once and then his eyes focused on the detective.

"Who?"

"We don't know."

"How?"

"She was on the pier with the woman detective we assigned to her for protection. You know how isolated it is out there. A fishing craft came up, a power boat about eighteen feet long. Marsha went out to talk to them, to tell them to keep away so they wouldn't harm the sensitive experiments in the water, and as she started to talk a submachine gun opened up. At least it was quick. She never knew what happened. Detective English got out the door and returned fire, six rounds, and she was hit in the shoulder and thigh. Marsha was dead immediately. At least fifteen rounds hit her, 9-mm Parabellum."

Mark stood and walked to the end of the bar, then back to the table. His face was frozen, *welded* into a grim, determined and deadly frown. He looked down at the detective.

"Thanks for telling me."

"Wilson, it's a police matter now, we'll handle it. One of our own was put down too."

"Do you have any one in custody?"

"No."

"Do you have any suspects?"

"Not at the moment. It only happened three hours ago."

"All right."

"Wilson, I know how you feel. She was an untainted, uninvolved innocent. Whoever killed her did it for revenge and out of anger and hatred. We can't drop to their level."

"Read your Bible, Sergeant. The good book says, "an eye for an eye, a life for a life." I probably won't be seeing you around."

"Wilson, I don't want to have to bring you in . . . for anything."

"Don't worry, Detective Jones, you'll never bring me in. You'll never see me again, and you can make book on that." Mark turned and walked out of the restaurant and faded into the parking lot where he crouched behind a car as the detective rushed out looking for him. Detective Jones waited for twenty minutes, checking each car that left the parking lot before he gave up and drove his unmarked tan police car out of the lot and down the drive toward the freeway below.

Mark made sure he was gone, then drove the other way into La Jolla. His computerlike mind had been evaluating the problem. Angie Lavangetti was the only suspect. She or some of her men had done it. She might not know about her brother yet. He would have to be found first. Mark phoned her number, which he remembered. Angie was out, but would be back for the evening.

Mark sorted through various methods for getting into the complex. He had been in before. It would better if he could catch her outside where she would have less protection. She would be on her guard after the hit. He had to go inside.

But he wanted her to be there when he went in. It would be a soft entry all the way. Mark got back into his car and drove to the La Jolla Towers, parked across the street and settled down to wait for her crew wagon to roll in. There was almost no way to miss it.

The dull ache drilled through him again. She was safe, he had beaten them, he had rescued her from a turkey death, and now they swept in with a boat and used a machine gun.

The silent, numbing rage surged over him again. It was much like what he had experienced when Donna Morgan had been murdered in that car crash; like what he had experienced every time an innocent died because of even a tenuous, obscure connection with him. It made him more determined than ever to wipe out this insanity, to clean out every last Mafia hoodlum and murdering bastard he could find. To provide instant justice on the end of a .45-caliber hollow-point round!

Mark let his hands relax. They had gripped the steering wheel until his fingers were white. It made him realize again that there was justice in the world only when men saw to it that there was justice. Each man had to stand up and fight for what was right and just and honest. Only then would there be a society where people were safe, where there was no crime, and where everyone helped and protected and *cared* for everyone else.

The black Caddy eased into the entrance and slid into the parking garage below the first-floor level. It was Angie, he had seen her in the back seat.

An eye for an eye.

Mark opened the weapons suitcase and took out what he would need. Two of the C-4 cherry bombs, the Ingram and the silencer, Ava on his hip with death dart loads. He slipped on a windbreaker that had "Ace Building Services" lettered on the back and took the identification card from the pocket and slid it in his shirt pocket. The Ingram went around his neck on a cord and the jacket concealed it. From the other suitcase he took out the small metal case with "Building Services" painted on the side. It was minimal soft-entry gear he had used before.

The Penetrator walked across the street and went in the front door. He spied the door man guard and waved.

"Sorry, man, I couldn't find no service entrance. Got an emergency call from some woman in 1112 who said get here right away, damn faucet dripping was driving her bananas. I told her it could wait until morning, to shut the door and go to sleep or turn up the TV sound, but no, no, she's got to have it fixed tonight. I tell her it'll cost her double time, and she says money isn't a problem. Where's your service elevator?"

The doorman sighed. "We don't have one, use the regular one. It's a crime the way some people act around here. Regular maintenance man would have done it tomorrow."

"Yeah, and how!" Mark waved and walked past the guard to the elevator, punched the "up" button and soon was on his way to the twelfth floor. He opened the windbreaker when he came to a stop and the doors rolled to each side. Mark swung up the chopper as he walked off the lift, and found only one bored soldier staring back at him.

"Don't reach for it, idiot," Mark hissed at him. "Take your piece out and lay it on the desk, then move down the hall in front of me. Any excuse and you're dead."

The Mafia hoodlum did as he was told. Mark pushed him through the first door.

"Show me which room Angie uses, the one she's in now."

He pointed two doors down and Mark prodded him forward.

"Hit the floor, slouch!"

The command came from down the hallway and when the hood fell to the floor, Mark swept the corridor with a six-round burst and heard a scream and then silence. Mark kicked the man below him and charged to the door he had pointed to. It was unlocked, and he found himself in a woman's sitting room, a living room, with soft colors, flowers in a vase, a small piano, TV set, and overstuffed expensive furniture. No one was there.

He ran to a door and kicked it open: A bath, empty.

The other door opened into a bedroom and he saw clothes strewn around but no Angie. The bedroom had a connecting door into an office, which was empty, but a second door out of the office led into the hall. Mark looked down the corridor and saw two gunmen. A pistol sounded and a round chipped the door molding over Mark's head.

Mark ducked back inside, put the Ingram around the door and sent ten rounds stuttering down the hall in silent destruction. One man screamed.

Then Mark knew. She had heard him come and run. The men were covering for her. Down the elevator to her car. He used the Ingram again, lacing five more rounds down the hallway as he ran toward the door he had come in, the one that connected to the elevators.

He almost made it before a man leaned from the first door to see what was happening. Mark shot him with Ava and roared past. Two lonesome shots came from the far end of the hall, but by that time Mark was through the door and racing down the stairwell. On the eleventh floor he punched up the elevator and hoped it was nearby. It must have been. The light flashed and the doors opened and he got on the empty car and hit the button for the garage-level stop.

The lift did not stop on the way down and when the doors opened in the garage parking area, he saw one car coming in, but none going out. Then an engine roared and a big crew wagon shot past him and toward the back of the structure. It would have to circle the building and come out the front entrance.

Mark ran flat out for his car across the street and barely got to it and had the engine started when the black Caddy shot out of the entrance and turned north. Mark gunned his Chevy into the street heading south, did a 180-degree sliding skid, headed north now, chasing the receding taillights of the Caddy.

The big car was easy to follow through town and then onto Torrey Pines Road. They were heading for Del Mar or points north. The road led out of La Jolla, past the heavily traveled section along UCSD, then traffic faded to almost nothing as the Caddy bored along North Torrey Pines Road, leading to the beach and Del Mar.

Mark leaned out the window and sent a scattering of five rounds at the Caddy's rear tires. He missed. As they were roaring down the grade toward the ocean, he used up the last rounds in the first magazine in the Ingram, and this time hit a tire, the Caddy swerved, was righted, and slowed dramatically. Mark jammed a second magazine into the Ingram and watched the Caddy come to a sliding halt at the side of the road two hundred yards from where the road met the beach at the end of the state park.

Two rounds slammed into Mark's rented car. The Penetrator stopped his rig fifty feet away and eased out the off side door. He sent five rounds through the Caddy's left front window and waited. There were no more return shots. Then Mark jumped up and saw a figure moving down the edge of the road. A woman.

He held the silenced Ingram and raced after the woman, it had to be Angie. She was tougher and faster than she looked. She had taken off her sandals and ran barefoot. Mark had to call on all of his speed to start catching up with her. She hit the beach area and plunged down the trail to the sand a dozen yards away, then came to the hard sand and ran fast south, toward the towering cliffs and the narrow band of sand now sandwiched between high tide and the bluffs.

She was tiring.

Twice she looked over her shoulder and in the faint moonlight he could see anger and fear on her pretty face. When she was two hundred yards up the beach and near the towering cliffs, she stopped and turned, watching him.

Mark came to a halt five yards away so he could see her plainly.

"Angie, why did you kill her?"

"Because you killed my men."

"She wasn't involved."

"Everyone is involved. Did you kill Carmine? They haven't found him yet."

"Yes, he *was* involved."

"Now I have to kill you," she said. She lifted a small-caliber handgun. Before she could aim he jolted forward, changed directions twice. She fired once and missed, fired again, and the round creased his shoulder, then he knocked the gun from her hand and threw it far out into the waves.

She fell to her knees in the soft sand.

"Were you in the boat at the Scripps pier?"

"Yes."

"Did you pull the trigger on the Ingram?"

"Does it matter?" She unbuttoned the top of the sleek dress she wore. "What does it matter, she's gone and I'm not. I'm alive and I know we will be good for each other. I've always dreamed of making love to you, Penetrator. You should have been a capo at least, then a don. You can do it all. You make people jump. You are extremely sexy." She peeled down the top of the dress and let it hang around her hips. Slowly she reached behind her back and unfastened her bra. He'd seen it all before on Black's Beach, but it was more interesting now as the white material slipped down, revealing her thrusting, full breasts with heavy brown nipples.

"Hey, take me on trial. Try me, you'll like me. If I'm not the best at what I do, then throw me out. I know how to make the stars and the moon move for you." She pulled the dress over her head and stood kicking out of a slip, and then hooked her thumbs in her brief panties, pushing them down her hips until they fell at her feet. She walked toward him, her smile radiant.

"Darling, we can be so good together, so deliciously good! You'll see. Now put down the silly guns and take off your clothes. There is something about making love on a public beach at night that gives it a special erotic flavor. Come on, sweetheart, let's take off your clothes." She held one hand in front of her as she walked to him. He lifted the muzzle of the silencer so it pressed between her breasts, stopping her.

"Did you shoot down Marsha Day?"

"What does it matter? You and I. . . ."

He grabbed her face with his big hand and squeezed her cheeks until she yelped in pain.

"Did you pull the trigger on that submachine gun?"

"Yes." The sound came out oddly past his hand. He relaxed his left hand and she smiled. "Now, darling, get rid of your old clothes and let's make marvelous, wonderful love, three times!"

She was beautiful, darkly perfect, with a glorious figure all his for the taking.

She smiled at him again and leaned in to kiss him, but the long silencer kept her away.

"Darling, please. I want you to poke me, but not with that gun."

He eased it upward slightly and she pushed closer to him. The Ingram now pointed at her chin.

In a move so silent and quick that it almost worked, she swung her right hand from behind her and the moonlight glinted off a six-inch knife blade. Mark's right finger caressed the Ingram trigger and twenty 9-mm Parabellum rounds slammed into Angie Lavangetti's chin, exploded upward through her mouth and into her brain, throwing her backward four feet and spraying the dry sand with a thousand droplets of blood, bone fragment, brain cells, hair, and cranial tissue.

18

For The Living

For a long moment the Penetrator stared at the lifeless, torn-apart form that had once been Angela Lavangetti. Her face was half blown away, her head a sticky mass of blood and hair. He took a deep breath and turned, walking back up the beach.

A cold wind whipped in and with the on-shore flow came mists and fog, then a silent, thin rain began to fall. He jogged up the road toward his car, stowed all of his weapons in his suitcase and put that in the trunk, then he drove ten miles up the beach to a small park, locked his car, and began running along the wet sand.

He was soon soaked through.

It didn't matter.

Marsha Day was dead. Her face floated to him out of the mists and he wished that somehow he had never met her, had never climbed out of the sea on her pier, had never talked to her that morning after Cully's death. Had never . . . had never. . . .

He screamed into the wetness of the night and kept running. The beach ended at a cliff and he went up a street following the shore until the open sand showed again.

He ran through the dark, wet night.

They were dead, all dead. Cully Ambrose, another innocent, and Carmine Lavangetti, Angie Lavangetti, and a dozen of their Mafia hoodlums. He was not weeping for the Mafia soldiers. They got what they had been earning for the last several years. They deserved death.

The Penetrator kept running.

By morning he was far up the beach, miles from his car. He wasn't sure where he was. Sometime during the night he had slowed to a walk, but he kept on. It was all churning around in his mind, punishing him for each death, sending him screaming down rivers of blood; it was chastising him for taking the human life he was so determined to protect.

But these people were not human; they were maggots, they were parasites, they were leeches sucking the life's blood from innocent Americans who could not protect themselves.

During the night, the *game*, the football aspect of the whole mission had paled into insignificance, almost into a ridiculous posture as he considered it logically. Grown men playing schoolboy games and getting paid for it! Stupid. And other grown men and women paying millions and millions of dollars each year to come watch the big men smash and crash and run into each other.

The hoodlums who conspired to fix the outcome of the games and the point spread seemed to be the most logical in the whole scenario. At least he understood them . . . and hated them.

Just after 7 A.M. Mark struggled into a café near a small industrial area, and a waitress with pink cheeks and sparkling blue eyes who was thirty pounds overweight brought him a hot cup of coffee without asking. She grinned at him, her eyes glowing with amusement and concern.

"Speaking of being all wet, you really are. Want to borrow a nice, soft, dry towel?"

He shook his head and turned away. No more. No more would he involve the innocents.

She frowned. "You sick, you hurt? Can I call somebody for you? Jesus, looks like you been out in the rain all night."

He shook his head again and sipped the coffee. He was tired enough, he might be able to sleep. He waved the girl away, not wanting to hurt her feelings, but rather that than her being dead one day.

He had two cups of coffee, then walked to a small, run-down motel and paid twenty-five dollars cash in advance for a room. He forgot what name he signed, then stumbled to the room and fell on the bed.

He slept ten hours, then paid thirty dollars for a taxi ride back to his car, and rented a better motel room where he had a shower and slept another ten hours.

Mark woke up still angry, furious at everyone, and drove to Mission Bay in San Diego, where he rented an eighteen-foot boat, fishing gear, and a twenty-gallon bait-saver tank full of anchovies to trail over the stern.

An hour later he was fishing off the Scripps pier.

He drifted in the gentle swells and stared at the pier. Mark pulled in a fish, a calico bass, carefully unhooked the fourteen-inch specimen and released it gently back to the sea.

Mark threw out another darting, frisky anchovy and watched it swim for the depths where it might find a school of its kind for protection. A two-foot-long barracuda slanted in and gulped down the anchovy hook and all and Mark played the fish up to his boat and then released it.

A soft rain came again. He went on fishing. Two hours later he had caught half a dozen different varieties of fish. He looked up at the pier. He had drifted south from it. The Penetrator nodded. "Thanks, Marsha, thanks for taking me fishing."

The Penetrator stowed his gear and started the motor. He could be back at the Stronghold before dark. Yes, he would enjoy the high desert again. The stillness, the hot dry air. And he should look over the future mission project board, see what was important, seek out another injustice that needed his attention. He couldn't be sitting around loafing this way.

The old spark of interest glowed within him. It wasn't dead after all. The Penetrator would live to fight another day. The closer he came to the dock in Mission Bay, the more interested he became in his new mission, whatever it might be.

There were several situations that were moving into the intolerable stage. He would ask the Professor his opinion and then pick another project. He had the quarter of a million dollars from the Las Vegas mob for the Professor to put into three or four local banks, spreading it out so no report of a large cash deposit would need to be made by the banks. Much of it they would keep in cash at the Stronghold to finance future operations.

Mark Hardin, the Penetrator, gunned the little motor and slid up to the dock in Mission Bay. He was ready and anxious to find a new project and, as the TV public-service commercial said, to "take a *bite* out of crime."

by Lionel Derrick
THE PENETRATOR